"Why is all of this...bad?" Becca asked.

"Because they're giving what they don't have."

"Many in our community have more than enough."

"And many don't." Daniel scrubbed his hands over his face. "Many don't, and they've given part of what little they have to me. That's not right because I—"

He stopped midsentence, a pained expression on his face.

"What? You had nothing here, Daniel. People wanted to help. Now, don't ruin it by letting your pride become involved."

"It's not pride."

"What is it, then?"

"I can't... I can't explain why this is such a terrible thing, Becca. Just trust me. I should not have accepted this much help."

He seemed to be stuck on the fact that he was poor.

Her family was poor, too, but they didn't mind having food and clothing and a furnished home.

Men were a mystery to her, and Daniel Glick? Daniel was a paradox. For a guy who carried around a book and filled it with words of wisdom, he had a lot of learning to do.

Vannetta Chapman has published over one hundred articles in Christian family magazines and received over two dozen awards from Romance Writers of America chapter groups. She discovered her love for the Amish while researching her grandfather's birthplace of Albion, Pennsylvania. Her first novel, *A Simple Amish Christmas*, quickly became a bestseller. Chapman lives in Texas Hill Country with her husband.

Books by Vannetta Chapman

Love Inspired

Indiana Amish Brides

A Widow's Hope
Amish Christmas Memories
A Perfect Amish Match
The Amish Christmas Matchmaker
An Unlikely Amish Match
The Amish Christmas Secret

Visit the Author Profile page
at Harlequin.com for more titles.

The Amish Christmas Secret

Vannetta Chapman

LOVE INSPIRED

INSPIRATIONAL ROMANCE

LOVE INSPIRED®
INSPIRATIONAL ROMANCE

Recycling programs
for this product may
not exist in your area.

ISBN-13: 978-1-335-42971-1

The Amish Christmas Secret

This edition published by arrangement with Harlequin Books S.A.

For questions and comments about the quality of this book, please contact us
at CustomerService@Harlequin.com.

Love Inspired
22 Adelaide St. West, 40th Floor
Toronto, Ontario M5H 4E3, Canada
www.Harlequin.com

Printed in U.S.A.

But my God shall supply all your need
according to his riches in glory by Christ Jesus.
—*Philippians* 4:19

Your wealth is where your friends are.
—Plautus

This book is dedicated to Kristy Kreymer.

Chapter One

❧

Daniel Glick moved into his new place on the first Tuesday in October. The next day, the local bishop—an old fellow named Saul Lapp who looked to be in his eighties—gave him a ride to Tim Beiler's place. Tim was apparently the go-to guy in Shipshewana, Indiana, if one was looking to purchase a buggy horse.

Daniel didn't even attempt to negotiate down the price of the mare. Constance was dark gray along her mane and from her hindquarters to her hooves. The rest of her coat was nearly silver. She was more muscled and longer bodied than the horse he'd owned in Pennsylvania, standing fifteen hands high and weighing in at 825 pounds. An American saddlebred, she was three years old and presented a nice gait. More important, her name perfectly matched her disposition.

He'd purchased the worst farm in Shipshewana.

His buggy looked as if it might not hold together in a good storm.

But he wouldn't skimp on the horse. The mare was fundamental to his new life in Indiana. She was the beginning of a twenty-year relationship. He'd gladly pay full price.

The bishop had dropped him off at Tim Beiler's place, assuring Daniel he had the best buggy horses in the area.

Tim Beiler looked to be in his late forties. With a salt-and-pepper beard, he was built like a fireplug and didn't even blink when he quoted a price several hundred above the high side for a good buggy horse.

"She's the best mare I have."

"I'll take her."

"*Gut.* You won't regret it." If Tim was surprised that Daniel didn't haggle the price, he hid it well.

Daniel counted out the bills, thanked the man and told him he'd ride her home. It wasn't often that he rode a horse, let alone bareback, but then again, it wasn't often in a man's life that he moved over five hundred miles to a place where he knew no one, and purchased a new horse.

He took his time on the way home, riding the horse along the side of the road, taking in the *Englisch* and Amish homes of Shipshewana, Indiana.

The October afternoon was bright with sunshine.

Fall flowers bloomed to his left and right.

Leaves crunched under Constance's hooves. She seemed to enjoy the sounds of fall and the freedom of the afternoon as much as Daniel did.

Soon the *Englisch* neighborhoods gave

way to picture-perfect farms. He turned west. Here the farms became smaller and noticeably poorer, largely because there wasn't sufficient top soil for farming. Most of Shipshe was quite fertile, but this area would be a challenge for the best of farmers.

The property he'd purchased was four and a half miles from the center of town and was in a marked state of disarray. Its condition suited Daniel to a tee. He wouldn't have to worry about *Englischers* pausing in their cars to take pictures.

Seclusion.

Peace.

Quiet.

Those things had been at the top of Daniel's list as he'd sought a property far from home. The Realtor had tried to persuade him to look at more expensive properties with "livable" homes. He hadn't shown the advertisements to his parents, but he could have guessed their reaction—surprise followed by disappointment. They expected him to make something of himself, especially given *their situation.*

"Unto whomsoever much is given, of him shall much be required." His *dat* loved to quote the verse from Luke's gospel. It was amazing to Daniel that he didn't see the hypocrisy in that. The inheritance they'd received had literally destroyed their family, and yet he would dare to lecture Daniel on how he should live his life.

The inheritance was the reason he'd left.

Call it running away or deserting his family or starting over. The name of it didn't matter so much as the fact of it. He was five hundred miles away from a life that had only yielded pain and betrayal. He hoped five hundred miles would be far enough.

He'd been looking for solitude when he purchased the place, and he had no doubt he'd find it here. As for the decrepit condition of his house and barn and fields, if there was one thing he didn't mind, it was a challenge.

Once home, he brushed down the mare, put oats in a bucket and hooked the bucket to the fence. Then he set her loose in the east pasture, which was the only portion of his farm that had a fence in good enough condition to hold her. Walking toward his barn, he nearly laughed. He shared it with a neighbor he hadn't met yet—the barn had been built directly on the property line. It was one more reason no one had been interested in the property. The structure looked as if a good wind would blow it down, and the house was no better.

He had the skill and the time to repair both.

But the horse he would keep in the pasture until the structure was sound.

He'd walked into the barn and was putting the brush on a shelf when he heard a high-pitched squeal from the other side of the wall. With every fiber of his being, he wanted to ignore it. He would meet his neighbors soon enough, but he had no desire to do so on the second night in his new place.

"Get back!"

Definitely a female voice, from the other side of the barn. Poisonous snakes were rare in Indiana, but it was possible that his neighbor had encountered a copperhead or timber rattler. He'd never forgive himself if she was bitten while he stood on his side of the barn enjoying his solitude.

He threw one glance back toward his home, then sighed and walked around the barn. If someone had asked him to guess what he might find there, he wouldn't in a hundred years have guessed correctly.

A young Amish woman—Plain dress, apron, *kapp*—was holding a feed bucket in one hand and a rake in the other, attempting to fend off a rooster. The rooster was a beautiful Brahma, over two feet tall, with a red comb and golden cape. At the moment, the bird was strutting and crowing and occasionally jerking to the right and left, trying to peck the woman's feet.

"What did you do to him?" Daniel asked.

Her head snapped up, and her eyes widened. The rooster took advantage of her inattention and made a swipe at her left foot. The woman danced right and once again thrust the feed bucket toward the rooster. "Don't just stand there. This beast won't let me pass."

Daniel knew better than to laugh. He'd been raised with four sisters and a strong-willed mother. Laughing was not the correct response when he saw a don't-mess-with-me look in a woman's eyes. So he strode forward, snatched the rooster up from behind, pinning its wings down with his right arm, and keeping its head turned away from him with his left hand.

"Where do you want him?"

"His name is Carl, and I want him in the oven if you must know the truth." She dropped the feed bucket and swiped at the golden blond hair that was spilling out of her *kapp.* "Over there. In the pen is fine."

The pen she pointed toward looked as if it had long ago held pigs. Given its current condition—it was as dilapidated as everything else—Daniel doubted whether it would keep Carl corralled for long. He dropped the rooster inside and turned to face the woman. She was probably five and a half feet tall, neither heavy nor thin, and looked to be around twenty years old. Blue eyes the color of forget-me-not flowers assessed him.

She was also beautiful in the way of Plain women, without the adornment of makeup or jewelry. The sight of her nearly brought a groan to his lips and reminded him of yet another reason why he'd left Pennsylvania. Why couldn't his neighbors have been an old couple in their nineties?

"You must be the new neighbor. I'm Becca Schwartz—not Rebecca, just Becca, because I was the second born and my *mamm* decided to do things alphabetically. We thought you might come over and introduce yourself, but I guess you've been busy. *Mamm* would want me to invite you to dinner, but I have to warn you, I have seven younger siblings, so it's usually a somewhat chaotic affair, and we're probably having soup same as every night this week seeing as how the price of hay has dropped again and hunting season hasn't started yet."

It was a lot of words.

As she talked, Becca not Rebecca had stepped closer. Daniel took a step back.

"Didn't catch your name."

"Daniel... Daniel Glick."

"We didn't even know the place had sold until last week. To say we were surprised would be a huge understatement. Thought Jeremiah was fooling with us— Jeremiah is my *onkel* on my *dat*'s side. He's a real prankster. So when he told us the place had sold, we didn't believe him at first. Most people are leery of farms where the fields are covered with rocks and the house is falling down. I see you haven't done anything to remedy either of those situations."

"I only moved in yesterday."

"Had time to purchase a horse, though."

They were standing outside the Schwartz side of the barn. Becca stepped past him, crossed her arms over the top of the fence and whistled twice.

Constance raised her head as if to nod and say hello, then went back to grazing.

"Nice mare."

"*Ya.*"

"Get it from Old Tim?"

"The man didn't strike me as terribly old."

"He's older than Young Tim but not as old as Timothy." Becca shrugged as if to say, *you know how it is.* "Hope you didn't pay what he was asking. He always starts high."

The last thing Daniel wanted was to get into a conversation about how he'd over-paid for the mare. What he wanted to do was walk away. He'd purchased eggs, bacon and bread when he was in town the day before, and his stomach was beginning to growl.

Then he glanced back at the barn.

The Realtor had explained that he owned half of it, which he hadn't taken the time to question. He stared at it now, wondering how to broach the subject or if Becca would even know the answers to his questions.

How did one own half a barn?

As if she could read his mind, she said, "The Coblentz *bruders* built it this way back when Shipshe was barely a dot on the map."

"It's barely a dot on the map now."

"They came from Ohio, purchased what they thought was two pieces of prime real estate that shared a property line. Built the barn so that each could use half and planned to build their houses in sight of one another. George Coblentz built your house, and Clarence had just begun to plan out his on what is now our side when they had their fight."

"Fight?"

"Over a woman, of course." Becca smiled broadly as if she found the whole story amusing. No doubt she'd told it a dozen times before. Her blue eyes literally twinkled.

If he were honest, she looked like an Amish woman that you might find on the cover of an *Englisch* tour brochure. Her hair was golden blond, prettier than wheat in the fields—not that he could see more than an inch of it. She had a button nose, the lightest dusting of freckles and a smile that should have been able to charm the bad-tempered rooster, Carl.

"Don't know the woman's name—"

"What woman?"

"The one the Coblentz *bruders* fought over."

"Ah."

"Don't even know if she was interested in either of the *bruders*, but the old folks will tell you that she left town before Clarence managed to lay the foundation for his house. Each *bruder* thought the other had driven her away. Clarence built the fence because he wasn't speaking to George and didn't want his cattle crossing over. The next year he built his house."

She tilted her pretty head toward a single-story home that looked as if it had been added onto with each additional child. "Neither stayed long. Clarence moved on to Wisconsin and George went back to Ohio."

"So the barn…"

"Is half yours, half ours."

"I've never owned half a barn before."

"Too bad Carl's on this half, as he's the most foul-tempered rooster I've ever encountered. *Gut* thing I brought him over to this barn, though. I don't believe my hens are ready to meet him yet."

"Your parents have another barn?"

"*Ya*, up past our house."

Daniel could just make out a structure

that looked to be in no better shape than the one they were standing beside.

"Why are you and Carl here and not in the…uh…newer barn?"

"My parents said I could use this one for my projects."

"Projects?"

Before Becca could answer, someone stepped out onto the front porch of her house and rang the dinner bell. "Sounds like the soup's ready. Care to come and meet the folks?"

"Another time. I have some…um…unpacking to do."

Becca shrugged her shoulders as if it didn't matter to her whether he joined them or not. "Guess I'll be seeing you, then."

"Yeah, I guess."

He'd hoped for peace and solitude.

He'd hoped to be left alone.

He'd prayed that he wouldn't have to deal with women for a year or longer.

Instead, he had half a barn, a cantankerous rooster, and a pretty neighbor who didn't mind being a little nosy.

What kind of projects did she have?

And how much time did she spend in the barn they shared?

None of which was any of his business. He'd come to Indiana to forget women and to lose himself in making something good from something that was broken. He'd moved to Indiana because he wanted to be left alone.

Meeting the neighbors was way down his to-do list.

Becca barely thought about the tall, handsome and largely silent Daniel Glick for the rest of the evening. She didn't dwell on his dark brown hair, brown eyes with a hint of gray, muscular frame or serious demeanor. Instead, she spent her time trying to figure out exactly what he was doing in Shipshe.

Unfortunately, her unruly family gave her little quiet for thinking. Dinner for ten was no easy affair. Clyde, David and Eli had to be reminded to knock the mud off their shoes before coming into the kitchen. Francine was mooning over a boy at school and burned the corn bread. Georgia had her nose in a book—Georgia always had her nose in a book, even when she was supposed to be stirring the soup, which had resulted in a nice crust on the bottom where it had stuck. As for Hannah and Isabelle, they'd tried to sneak in two of the barn cats in their apron pockets.

Things were quiet for exactly thirty seconds of the meal, while the entire family joined hands and silently prayed. After that, the chaos quickly returned. Her *dat* loved to tell jokes during dinner. She couldn't imagine where he got them from, but he seemed to have an endless supply and delighted in sharing them.

"What did the baby corn ask the mama corn?" He grinned mischievously as he spread butter on Hannah's corn bread.

"I know," Hannah declared.

Isabelle shook her head, causing her *kapp* strings to bounce and nearly land in her soup. "No, you don't."

"I could guess."

"Then guess already."

"I don't know, then. I forgot."

Hannah and Isabelle were at the age where they were either arguing or sitting with their heads so close together that they appeared to be physically joined. Theirs was a tumultuous relationship, but *Mamm* declared that was normal for twins, especially five-year-old twins.

"The baby corn leaned close to the mama corn and asked...where's popcorn?" Her *dat* laughed at his own joke, oblivious to the fact that Becca had rolled her eyes, and Clyde and David had both groaned quite loudly.

The twins giggled, though, and soon her siblings were discussing what corn would say if it really could talk. Dishes were passed back and forth, three different spills were cleaned up, and in general, pandemonium was once again the word of the day.

To be honest, Becca didn't mind too much.

She'd learned to tune most everyone and everything out when she was focusing on something, and at the moment she needed time to ponder her new neighbor.

Who was Daniel Glick?

Why had he bought that tumbling-down excuse for a farm?

Assuming he couldn't afford a better farm—because who would buy something terrible if they could afford something good—how did he have enough money for the mare? The mare was a real beauty. Becca planned to go back over the next day and take a closer look.

She mulled several possible scenarios in her head through dinner. Before she knew it, everyone was darting off to finish chores or spend a few minutes outside as the sun set. She washed and dried the dishes by herself, which she preferred because it gave her time to think. Kitchen cleanup was one of the very rare quiet times in their home, since everyone scattered rather than get dragged into the chore. Becca dried the last spoon, hung the dish towel on the hook and stepped out on the front porch to enjoy the end of the day.

The sun was just beginning to set, casting long shadows across the fields. She could almost pretend that they lived on a beautiful farm, with rows of flowers surrounding their vegetable garden, a large new barn and at least three buggies.

Their farm wasn't beautiful.

They'd not been able to afford flowers again this year, and their vegetable garden had been harvested weeks ago.

As for the buggy, they had exactly one and it seemed to be on its last wheel.

Her quiet assessment of their living conditions—something her mind insisted on turning to, time and again—was interrupted all too quickly.

"You were quiet during dinner tonight." Her *mamm* was sitting in the porch rocker and hemming a dress, probably for Hannah or Isabelle, by the size of it.

Becca wasn't sure she'd ever seen her mother just rest. She always seemed to be sewing or darning or knitting or cooking or cleaning.

"I was?"

"You don't have to talk about it if you don't want to."

"Talk about what?"

"Whatever's on your mind."

"You'd think that in a family as big as ours, some things would go unnoticed."

"Is that what you want? Not to be noticed?"

Becca sighed and turned from the porch railing to face her *mamm*. "I met our neighbor today."

"Did you, now?"

"Have you met him?"

"*Nein.* Your *dat* told me he saw a young man moving in yesterday, or rather he saw

Bishop Saul drop him off at the place. Apparently, the man didn't come with any furniture."

"A mystery wrapped in an enigma."

"It is hard to imagine who would have bought it—that place has been empty a very long time." She shifted the garment on her lap and continued hemming. "It will be *gut* to have neighbors again."

"Oh, I'm not sure you'll feel that way about Daniel Glick."

"And why would you say that?"

Becca walked over to the adjacent rocker and perched on the edge of the seat, lowering her voice as if to share a secret—though there was no one else on the porch and she didn't actually know any secrets about Daniel. "He's not very…how do I say this? He's not particularly friendly."

"How so?"

"Oh, I don't know. Usually, people tell you something about where they came from or why they moved to an area. I talked to the man for ten minutes, and

I can't tell you anything more than his name. Oh, and he bought a mare—a beautiful mare—from Old Tim."

"I hope he didn't pay too much."

"Probably he did, because I said the same thing and he got all stiff and put-out-looking."

"Hmm."

"Also, I invited him to dinner, but he said he had unpacking to do."

"Curious."

"Where's he even staying? You know as well as I do that the house is about to fall in on itself. I'm sure there are holes in the roof, and the floor was rotten in places last time I walked through it."

"You walked through the Coblentz place?"

Becca waved away her concern. "Years ago. Abigail and I were playing hide-and-seek on that side of our property, and I thought it would be super smart to hide in the old house. I'm lucky a rat didn't bite my ankle."

"You two girls certainly did know how to get in trouble."

"The boys were just as bad."

"You're not wrong." Her *mamm* tied a knot in her thread, then snipped it with a tiny pair of scissors. "Perhaps Saul will schedule a workday."

"What would that accomplish? Unless you're saying we should pull down Daniel Glick's house and start over. Now, that might make sense."

Which seemed to sum up all they could think of to say about their new neighbor.

Becca was about to get up and check on her hens when her mother asked about the new rooster. Sighing and sinking back into the rocker, she described how the beast had tried to attack her, and how Daniel had come to her rescue.

"Now you know why the Grabers gave him away."

"Molly Graber told me as much, but I didn't believe her."

"You didn't really need a rooster. You're

making *gut* money with the eggs from your hens."

"Not really, only $3.50 a dozen."

"What made you think you wanted to raise chickens?"

"Because I read this book…"

"I should have guessed that."

"The book said that *Englischers* will pay for organically raised chickens."

"Meaning what exactly?"

"You know—organic. Natural. Like pretty much everything around here." Becca tapped her fingers against the arm of the rocker, trying to remember exactly what the book had said. "Let's see…no chemicals or steroids…"

"We definitely don't have any of that."

"No GMO."

"I don't even know what that is."

"There was a bunch of other stuff." What had the book said about natural breeding and raising? She might have to check it out again because suddenly she was drawing a blank. "I do know that they said I could get $10 to $25 a chick, and that I could also sell the manure and the feathers."

"All you need is for Carl to cooperate."

"Exactly. He's a Brahma, and they're supposed to be docile."

"You don't say."

"Apparently no one has told Carl that. He's an ornery creature. I don't dare let him out of the pens in the old barn."

At that moment there was squawking and crowing, followed by Carl strutting into the yard and proceeding to chase one of the barn kittens. Hannah and Isabelle were chasing the rooster, and Cola the beagle was circling the entire group, barking with a loud voice that seemed to say, "Hey, hey, hey."

"Sounds as if your rooster escaped the old pens, dear."

Becca didn't bother to respond. She was already running down the porch steps and across the yard, wondering what she could use to catch Carl and what she was going to do with him after she did catch him.

Roosters were definitely more challenging than they'd described in the book; at least this rooster was. The book had definitely said that he'd be gentle and attentive to the hens. Ha! Her hens would lose all their feathers after one look at Carl.

Maybe the book was wrong.

Maybe the author didn't know what she was talking about.

Or maybe the author had never met a rooster quite like Carl.

Regardless, Becca's plan to make pockets full of money from selling organic chickens seemed to fade before her eyes. There had to be a way she could help her family financially. There had to be something she could do that would allow them to set a little bit of money back instead of simply getting by from week to week. That never seemed to bother her *mamm*—who stayed too busy with her daily chores to notice—or her *dat*, who would simply wink if she brought it up, and go on to tell another joke.

Becca hurried after Carl-the-bad-tempered-rooster. She thought that should be his full official name. The rooster wouldn't be her first project that didn't work out, but she wasn't going to let that stop her. She vowed for the hundredth time that she would find a way to lift her family out of abject poverty. But she might have to come up with a better idea than organic chickens.

Perhaps Daniel would be willing to go in on a project with her. By the looks of his situation, he could use additional funds as much as they could. The only problem was, he'd been quite standoffish.

She'd have to think of him as one of her projects.

All she needed to ensure his help was a good plan.

Chapter Two

Daniel spent Wednesday checking and mending the fence line in the east pasture. The last thing he needed was to see Constance trotting down the road without him. Spending time in the pasture with her also allowed him to get to know the mare. She was skittish at first, watching him out of the corner of her eye. By the end of the day, though, she was following him along the fence line—grazing within a few steps of wherever he was working.

Constance. He suspected that if he looked up the word in a dictionary, he'd find it meant steadfast or faithful. The mare seemed to be all of that and more. She was the exact opposite of the people who had been in his life up to this point. Animals could be trusted.

They didn't deceive.

Didn't pretend to feel something they didn't.

Didn't have ulterior motives.

With a determined effort, he pushed thoughts of the past away and focused on the moment in front of him.

"We're going to get along just fine." He ran a hand down the mare's neck and felt her relax. They were becoming used to one another—him and Constance. They made a good team. He planned to spend an hour each evening with her—checking her hooves, brushing her coat and generally working to help her grow accustomed to his presence.

Much to his dismay, that same hour seemed to coincide with the time Becca puttered around in the old barn. He made a concerted point of staying in the field with the mare rather than bringing her into her stall. That didn't succeed in keeping Becca on her side of the fence. She had no problem joining him and asking intrusive questions about his day.

Was he planning to redo the house? Yes, of course.

When? Soon.

Did he miss his family? Some.

Why wasn't he married?

Yes, she'd actually asked him that. Instead of answering, he'd deftly changed the subject. "How are you doing with Carl?"

"I've renamed him."

"Have you, now?"

"He's officially Carl-the-bad-tempered-rooster."

"I take it things aren't going well, then."

If he'd thought he could aggravate her into leaving, he was sorely mistaken. She'd simply taken the horse brush out of his hand and begun stroking Constance. "Carl may not work out."

"Tell me you're not thinking of eating him." He hoped she noticed the sarcasm in his voice, but if she did, she didn't show it. In fact, her expression turned quite serious.

"Oh, I might. This is a farm, and I have no problem adding that rooster to *Mamm*'s pot. *Nein*. It's more that I hate to give up on him. I keep thinking there might be one more thing I can try that will tame his unruly spirit."

"Such as?" In spite of his vow to avoid Becca Schwartz at all costs, Daniel found himself pulled into the details of her crazy scheme. He'd already heard about organic chickens and how much money she could earn if Carl would simply settle down and cozy up with the hens.

"I've yet to teach Carl his spot in the pecking order."

"Which is?"

"Below me!" Becca squirreled up her nose. "The problem is that he sees me as a trespasser."

"In the chicken coop?"

"I can't keep him in that thing. Did you see him earlier? He was chasing me across the field."

He had seen that and couldn't have held in his laughter if he'd tried. Fortunately, Becca had been too far away to hear him.

"I visited with Irma Bontrager this morning. If you haven't met her, she's our neighbor to the north. Anyway, Irma raised some prize-winning hens and roosters in her day."

"And what advice did Irma give you?"

"Wear knee-high rubber boots."

"Do you have a pair of those?"

"Of course not." She raised the hem of her skirt enough to reveal her calves. "Kneepads—fortunately they're a bit large on me and stretch nearly to my ankles. My *bruder* David—he's easy to pick out of our brood because he's always on his bike—he used to do quite a bit of in-line skating when he was younger. Said I could have them."

She nodded toward the rake she'd been holding the day before. "Irma also said to keep a weapon handy, and I'm to stomp and stare if he attempts to attack."

His mind flashed back on her running across the field, being chased by Carl. "Has that worked?"

"Not yet. Irma also said some roosters won't train, so I shouldn't be too hard on myself."

"Are you? Too hard on yourself?" Daniel wasn't sure why he was asking. He didn't need to know every little detail of Becca's life, but at the same time he was curious about what she'd say or do next.

"I don't think I am. I want things to work out, but if they don't, I always have a next plan."

"A next plan?"

"Yup." She looked as if she was about to say more, then clamped her mouth shut and continued brushing the mare.

Which technically was Daniel's job.

* * *

Thursday he decided that work on the house could wait. He didn't really mind sleeping outside on the back porch, and he probably had a couple of weeks before the weather turned cold.

Constance, on the other hand, needed a good solid stall.

He was on top of the barn's roof, pulling off shingles and rotted boards, when a buggy pulled into his yard. A tall, middle-aged man hopped out of the buggy and stood with his head back, hand shading his eyes, assessing Daniel's work.

"Beautiful day to reroof a barn."

"It is."

"Mind if I come on up?"

Daniel was a bit surprised at the question, but he waved him toward the south side of the barn, where he'd propped the ladder. The man scampered up quick as a cat and was soon perched on the side of the roof next to him. He was tall and thin, with a brown beard that was only slightly tinted with gray. The eyes were what gave him away—blue eyes the exact same shade as Becca's.

"Name's Samuel... Samuel Schwartz. We own the other half of your barn."

Daniel simply nodded.

Three days ago, that statement would have floored him, but he'd decided to accept the situation since he couldn't change it. He was tempted to offer to buy Samuel's half so he wouldn't have to deal with chatty girls and crazed roosters, but he was supposed to be poor. It might start rumors if he waved a wad of money at his neighbor the first time he met him.

"I've been meaning to put a new roof on this barn for years, but every time I'd get a little ahead, another *boppli* came along...not that I'm complaining. Sarah and I have nine *kinder*, and I wouldn't mind one more. There's something about holding an infant in your arms..."

Daniel knew nothing of that, so he turned the conversation back toward the barn. "I thought I'd repair the whole roof since it doesn't make much sense to patch half of it."

"But…"

"It was something I planned for when I bought the place… Financially, I mean."

"Roofing isn't cheap. You're sure you can afford this?"

He was going to have to think about how to explain things to folks without raising questions. From the look on Samuel's face, he could tell that what he was saying made no sense to the man. He'd purchased a farm that hadn't been productive in many years. The fences were falling down, pastures were overrun with thistles and weeds and rocks, and the house was plainly uninhabitable. Yet, here he was saying that he could afford to roof both halves of the barn.

When he'd first cooked up this plan to disappear, he'd promised himself that he would retain his integrity. He had vowed that he wouldn't lie to anyone, but now he understood that was going to be difficult unless he was willing to disclose how wealthy he was.

And that he was not willing to do.

He knew firsthand that such knowledge only brought trouble.

If he couldn't lie, and he couldn't tell the truth, he'd have to just stay silent on certain subjects.

Samuel had given up waiting for an answer. He reached down and pulled up a rotten board. "Doesn't seem right, though—your paying for my half."

He tossed the board onto the pile on the ground, turned to Daniel and smiled. "While I don't have any extra money lying around to help with the cost of materials, I do have two sons who are hard workers."

"Oh, I don't—"

"I'd come myself, but I told my *bruder* I'd help at his place. My boys—Clyde and David—are *gut* workers. They'll be here first thing tomorrow morning. Assuming you were planning on working on it again tomorrow."

"I'll be working on it."

"Gut!" Samuel pushed his hat down on his head and stood to go. He'd made it back to the ladder and started down when he stopped and called out again. "Almost forgot that Sarah sent me over to invite you to Sunday dinner."

Daniel managed to stifle a groan.

"I can see by your expression that you're wanting to say no, but that probably wouldn't be wise. She'd just show up on your doorstep with a basket of food. From the looks of your porch, she might fall through if she attempted to knock on your door."

"I was planning to get to that next."

"No man can do nothing and no man can do everything."

Daniel had no idea how to answer that, so he shrugged.

"We usually eat at noon on off-Sundays." With a nod, Samuel Schwartz disappeared below the roofline, only to pop back up again. "Why did the police arrest the turkey?"

"I have no idea. Why did the police arrest the turkey?"

"They suspected it of fowl play!"

Daniel could hear Becca's father laughing to himself as he walked toward his horse and buggy.

The horse was a chestnut gelding. Even as far away as he was, Daniel could see gray around his eyes and muzzle. He guessed the horse's age at fifteen or older, and he wondered why Samuel hadn't purchased a newer one. But then the man had said that he had nine *kinder* and no extra money. Daniel couldn't help but smile when Samuel pulled a piece of carrot out of his pocket and fed it to the horse before climbing back up in the buggy.

The buggy itself looked to be in as bad a shape as Daniel's—the rear driver's side had been dented in, and there was a long scrape down the passenger side, as well. Did they have another newer horse and buggy? There was no way the entire Schwartz family would all fit in the one Samuel was driving, so the family must have another. Otherwise, how would they get to church meetings?

None of which was his problem.

He wasn't going to get involved with the Schwartz family. He'd tried helping folks before, and every single time the situation had ended up worse than when he'd first become involved.

Nein.

He wouldn't be repeating that mistake here in Shipshewana.

Hadn't he come here to start over and put all of his past, including his new-found wealth—*especially* his newfound wealth—behind him?

Daniel turned his attention back to the roof, wishing with all his might he could finish it before Becca's brothers showed up to help.

* * *

It turned out that Clyde and David were excellent workers. They had their father's good nature but weren't as chatty as their older sister. Clyde was eighteen and worked on an *Englisch* farm three days a week. David was sixteen and thrilled not to be going back to school. He was happy to do anything that didn't involve a textbook. "For now I help my *dat*, but I'm hoping to find a real job this winter."

Both boys were tall and thin like their father.

They'd arrived as the sun was breaking the horizon Friday morning. Unfortunately they weren't alone. Becca was with them. At first he was afraid she planned to stay and help, but she put his mind to rest with a wave of her hand. "I'm not good on ladders."

"*Ya*. Remember the time you fell out of the tree house?" Clyde nudged David. "Thinking of one of her business plans and missed the last two steps. Had to walk in one of those boots for a month."

Becca turned away from her *bruders* and toward Daniel, thrusting a large basket in his hands.

"What's this?"

"Lunch—thick homemade bread and peanut butter spread, some oatmeal cookies and a large jug of raspberry-flavored tea. *Mamm* sent extra for you. Said you couldn't possibly have time to cook with all that needed to be done here."

Daniel felt guilty taking their food, but he couldn't think of a reason to turn it down that they'd accept.

"Tell her thanks."

"You can tell her yourself, when you come for dinner Sunday."

He closed his eyes and tried to think of a reason why he couldn't accept the invitation, which only caused Becca to laugh.

"I was surprised when *Dat* said you'd be there, knowing how much you like your privacy..."

"It was a goal when I moved here."

"And how you've avoided meeting my entire family..."

"*Avoid* is a strong word, since I've been here less than a week."

"But there you have it. You can look forward to an excellent meal, my *dat*'s jokes, and answering everyone's questions about why you moved to Shipshe."

She was definitely antagonizing him, and she was doing it on purpose. It was time he shifted the attention away from himself, so he stepped closer to her and said, "Maybe I'll hear more Becca stories. Tell me again how you fell out of the tree house."

Becca pressed her fingers to her lips, but a laugh still escaped. "You're pretty intent on keeping the focus off yourself, but that won't work with me. Maybe you'll have better luck with my parents."

She sashayed away before he could come up with a good retort. Becca Schwartz was free-spirited, excessively energetic, and irritating. She seemed bent on pulling him out of his shell. Well, good luck with that. He happened to like the shell he'd built around himself.

Then he looked up and saw Clyde and David waiting on top of his barn's roof. So much for being alone.

He'd removed a good bit of the roof the day before. Working together, the three of them were able to finish pulling off the rest of it in a couple of hours, and they started laying new cross boards before lunch. They were eating underneath the maple tree when Clyde asked him about the horse. "She's a beauty. What's her name?"

"Constance."

"*Gut* name," David said. "Our horse should be named Lazy."

David and Clyde laughed at that, though neither seemed particularly upset about the old horse or the condition of their buggy.

"We only have the one, but since it's all we've ever had we're used to it," Clyde said.

David mentioned riding his bike most places. "It's a problem if the weather turns bad, but we make it work."

To say they were good-natured was an understatement.

Daniel tried to remember a time when he'd been as content as Becca's *bruders* seemed to be, but he couldn't. Which proved that money didn't solve every problem. If it did, he'd be the happiest man in town.

If it did, he wouldn't have needed to move.

By the time the sun had begun to set, they'd repaired all of the rotted sections and begun hammering on shingles.

"Should be able to finish this tomorrow." David swiped at the sweat running down the back of his neck.

"Good thing, too, since rain is coming next week."

"Wouldn't want Constance in the rain."

"She's going to love her new digs."

Daniel tried to tell them that they'd done enough, that they didn't need to return the next day, but David and Clyde only smiled and said they'd see him in the morning.

Daniel was so tired that his legs felt like lead and his arms actually ached. He'd turned thirty the previous spring. He didn't consider himself old, but he also hadn't replaced a roof in a long time. The truth was that if he hadn't had David and Clyde helping, it would have taken him much longer. Clyde scampered up and down the ladder like a well-trained monkey, and David toted stacks of shingles as if they weighed nothing.

It had been a long day, a *gut* day, and Daniel was satisfied with what they'd managed to accomplish.

He cared for Constance, then went to the back porch and made a supper of instant oatmeal, coffee and toast—all done over an old camp stove. He forced himself to boil more water and wash up before collapsing into his sleeping bag. The bag was rated to twenty degrees, and the evening's temperature was nowhere near that. Lying there on his back porch, looking out at the stars, Daniel was in many ways happier than he'd been in a long time.

The quiet of the evening felt like a blessing poured over his soul.

The air was clean and crisp, and he felt as if he could breathe again for the first time in a long time.

But his mind insisted on tossing around questions for which he had no answer.

How did Becca's family cope with so little?

What was behind her insatiable curiosity about his past?

Why did the Schwartz family seem so satisfied—even in their poverty?

He thought of what Samuel had said. *No man can do nothing and no man can do everything.* He wasn't sure he understood it exactly, though the words had the ring of truth to them. He fetched his backpack and pulled out the notebook he often wrote in. Copying down the line, he studied it for a moment, then sighed, closed the book and stored it back in his bag.

As he tossed and turned, his mind returned again and again to his neighbors.

What was he going to do about pretty Becca Schwartz, who found an excuse to visit the barn every day?

And how was he going to maintain a distance between himself and the rest of the community, between himself and his neighbors? Because above all else, Daniel was determined to live a private life. He didn't want to develop friendships that would cause more heartache, and he certainly didn't want anyone attempting to fix him up with one of the local girls.

Dating and friendship were fine for other people.

But Daniel had learned firsthand that they wouldn't work for him. Friends would learn of his money, and then they would expect him to help—which he was only too happy to do. The problem was that when money became part of the equation, friendships took on a false tone. Too soon, strangers would be showing up at his place asking for a handout. Reporters would come by wanting to write about the Amish millionaire.

There was no end to it.

There was no peace in it.

He was better off alone, which was the way he planned to stay. His attempts to date since receiving his inheritance had been disastrous. *Nein.* He was better off without the heartbreak, even if it meant he occasionally felt lonely. He tossed onto his left side, his hip digging into the porch floor and a part of him wondering if he could sneak a new mattress into the house.

Becca Schwartz would notice.

She'd probably tell him he'd paid too much for it.

He almost laughed aloud at that. She was a spunky one. He'd give her that. The little that he'd seen of her had convinced him she was a hard worker, and it wasn't because she wanted to buy a new handbag or an *Englisch* phone. No, all Becca had mentioned when she was talking about her problem with Carl-the-bad-tempered-rooster was earning money for Clyde to purchase a buggy or her desire to buy the twins new coats. She cared about her family, that was for sure and certain.

It seemed to him that the *gut* women were already taken, and the ones—like Becca—who were looking for a better life, he had no business becoming involved with. The last few years had taught him they were after his money and not interested in him as a person.

No, the money he'd inherited had erected a wall between him and everyone else, and he didn't know how to climb over or move around it.

But he didn't need to.

He only needed peace and quiet to live out his own life.

And if he had to pretend to be poor in order to do that, he was happy to do so.

Becca had been over to Daniel Glick's place every day, and she'd yet to have a meaningful conversation with the man. He was plainly not interested in sharing any details about his life.

Which was fine.

She'd been brushed off before, and she didn't take it personally. She did enjoy working on puzzles, though, and there was definitely a mystery surrounding Daniel. She meant to solve it. So she plied her *bruders* with questions, though they could tell her very little. You'd think they'd have paid more attention, working with the man for two full days.

He slept on his back porch.

He was using an old camping stove to cook on.

He seemed to be every bit as poor as they were—though there was the horse.

The horse was a beauty. How had he been able to afford it?

Daniel had managed to avoid her when he was on the roof and she was in the pens. She'd relocated Carl inside the old barn and was attempting to introduce one of her hens to the rooster. All she'd accomplished was to receive a peck on her left ankle—directly below the borrowed kneepads. Carl had so traumatized Becca's hen that the bird had lost a good bit of her feathers.

She'd caught Daniel watching her as she'd shooed Carl back into the stall where she was now keeping him. She tossed a handful of feed at the rooster.

"Tell me you're not laughing at me, Daniel Glick."

Instead of answering, he'd simply tipped his hat and asked her *bruder* to grab more shingles.

Yes, Daniel was avoiding her quite successfully, which was easy enough to do when he was on the roof of the barn. He wouldn't get away so easily during the Sunday meal. There was little that Becca enjoyed more than solving the unsolvable. Her *dat* had once said she was worse than a hunting dog on point. In other words, there was no distracting her once she set her mind to a thing.

Sunday arrived overcast and warm—a sure sign that the rain they'd been predicting would arrive the next day.

Her *mamm* had invited Bishop Saul and the elderly neighbors whose farm sat just to their north—Irma and Joshua Bontrager. The Bontragers had grown children over in Goshen. They were always talking about selling their farm and moving to a *Daddi Haus* on their oldest son's place, but so far, no For Sale sign had appeared on their property.

The group was rounded out with Becca's older *schweschder*, Abigail, Abigail's husband, Aaron, and their two boys—William and Thomas.

"You're bigger this time." Becca placed

a hand against her *schweschder*'s stomach. "Tell him to move so I can feel it."

"Doesn't work that way. Babies tend to move in the middle of the night."

"Stubborn—like both of your other boys."

"Stop saying that. It could be a girl this time."

"Uh-huh." Becca turned back to the kitchen counter and resumed placing thick slices of ham on the platter.

"Find out anything more about your new neighbor?"

"*Nein.*"

"But you have a theory."

"I have several, but I can't prove any of them."

Abigail sat down at the table. She was putting peanut butter spread on the bread and slicing it into triangles for the *kinder*.

"He could be undercover Amish." Becca felt foolish suggesting such a thing, but hadn't she read in the newspaper about an undercover drug agent posing as an

Amish man? Or maybe she'd read it in a novel from the library. Regardless, she was glad to discuss the mystery of Daniel Glick with someone.

"Undercover? What does that mean?"

"You know...someone who is *Englisch*, a city slicker, who is merely pretending to be Amish."

"Why would someone do that?"

"I don't know. Maybe he's trying to ferret out a drug dealer."

"We don't have any drug dealers—at least none that I'm aware of. Though we did have that one boy selling his ADHD medicine at the local high school. I read about it in the paper last week. I don't know what the world is coming to."

"But back to Daniel..."

"I don't think your new neighbor is a police officer—undercover or not. For one thing, if he was, he wouldn't catch any criminals on his farm. You said yourself that he rarely leaves it, so..." Abigail let her sentence fade as she rearranged the sandwich quarters on the tray.

"I suppose you're right, but that doesn't mean he's simply a farmer." Becca snapped her fingers. "He could be in the witness protection program."

"Witness to what? And why would he need protection?"

"I don't know." Her friend Liza had a cell phone, one with access to the internet. They sometimes watched videos together—short silly things, but some of them had been about witnesses for high-profile trials being placed in federal custody in absurd places. "You have to admit that old farm would certainly be a *gut* place to hide someone."

Abigail proceeded to add slices of apple to the tray. "You said he was replacing his barn's roof…"

"Could be part of his cover story."

"And you mentioned that he was *gut* with the horse."

"Lots of people are *gut* with horses—

cowboys from Texas or Colorado or Montana."

"You read too many novels." Abigail sat back and rested her hand on her protruding stomach. "Also, he knew how to catch your rooster. I doubt a city slicker would know how to do something like that."

"Fine. Then maybe he is Amish, but he's on the run from the law."

"That's a terrible thing to think of someone."

"Maybe he got involved with the wrong people, and he didn't know how to get out of the mess, so he hightailed it out of there, flew the coop, headed for the hills."

"You certainly haven't lost your imagination."

Becca added slices of cheese to her platter, then covered it with a dish towel and sat down beside her *schweschder*. "You have to admit it's curious."

"What's curious?"

"Buying the worst place in town."

"I don't know if it's all that bad."

"Name one place in worse shape than Daniel Glick's farm."

Abigail stared up at the ceiling a minute, then shook her head. "Okay. You might be right about that part."

"He moved in with nothing more than a backpack."

"Men don't consider furniture a necessity."

"Which is a stereotype that doesn't always prove true. Your husband was the one who insisted on a new couch."

"New to us, but remember we bought it at a garage sale."

"And if Daniel really is poor..."

"*Mamm* would say that money isn't a necessary ingredient for happiness. She would say, *Where love is, there riches be...*"

"Okay, but the only love at Daniel Glick's place is between him and that mare. Don't you find that just a little odd? I heard from Molly, who heard from Old Tim's cousin, that he sold the mare at top price. Tell me how Daniel was able to afford that, but spends his evenings in a sleeping bag on the back porch?"

Abigail raised her hands in mock surrender. "I don't know. I'll admit it's curious, but it isn't a crime. You need to remember that men think differently than women. Most men—Amish and *Englisch*—care more about how they get from point A to point B than they do about where they sleep."

Which was an observation Becca couldn't argue with.

Her own *bruder* was saving every dime he made so that he could purchase a buggy. It would come in handy for courting, but of course, a buggy required another horse. He would rather put back what little money he had in the hopes of finding a cheap buggy and inexpensive horse than spend it on something more practical like new clothes. His old clothes had been mended several times, and the hem let down more than once.

"I still look like me in anything I wear," Clyde had said with a laugh. "But no girl likes to be picked up for a date on a bicycle."

The Sunday lunch passed in its usual way—pandemonium punctuated by her father's jokes, and of course both laughter and tears from the children. Abigail's youngest was in the midst of the terrible-two stage. Thomas had insisted on eating ham with no bread. He commenced to cry because he couldn't cut his meat, then cried because his *dat* cut it for him. Which merited another riddle from Becca's father—who thought he could make anyone laugh with a well-told joke.

"What animal can you always find at a baseball game?" He combed his fingers through his beard, then leaned forward and lowered his voice as if he were sharing a secret. "A bat!"

Becca didn't want to laugh, but she couldn't help it when her *dat* cackled at his own punch line.

"Life is *gut, ya*?" He reached over and mussed his grandson's hair.

Thomas glanced up at his grandfather and smiled. The cut meat was forgotten for a moment, then he glanced down, frowned at his plate, pushed a forkful of ham into his mouth and said, "I want to play baseball."

Several times throughout the meal, Becca caught Daniel sitting back and watching them. He said little, though he answered pleasantly enough when someone spoke directly to him.

His manners were good.

He'd found a way to clean up, though her *bruders* had said there was no working plumbing at his house.

He managed to answer questions about his family without giving away any real information. They lived in Lancaster. He didn't expect them to visit anytime soon. He'd picked Shipshewana because he'd heard it was a *gut* Amish community— not too strict and not too liberal. Daniel laughed with everyone else when he admitted, "And the price for the farm was right."

At different points in the meal, her *dat*, Abigail's husband, Aaron, Joshua Bontrager and Bishop Saul all mentioned stopping by to help. Each time Daniel managed to change the conversation. Becca paid attention to all of this, and she'd assembled a whole list of questions in her mind for when she managed to corner him.

She didn't have to wait long.

She'd gone to check on her hens. Cola the beagle dogged her feet, hoping she was carrying a treat in her pocket. She wasn't sure why she spoiled the dog so. Cola wasn't even purely a beagle, but rather some conglomeration of other breeds with beagle-like ears. There was something about the way those ears flopped over and her eyes glanced up in hope that caused Becca to squat, pet the dog, and pull a small biscuit out of her pocket. Cola accepted it gratefully, then rolled over onto her back to show her tummy.

"One scratch. I have chickens to check on."

She came around the corner of the barn to find Daniel staring into the chicken coop.

"Want to buy a chicken?"

"Are you selling?"

"I might be if the price was right."

"You're a real little entrepreneur, aren't you?" Daniel turned to study her. With his thumbs tucked under his suspenders and his hat tipped back on his head, he looked like he'd stepped off the cover of an Amish romance novel. Not that she read Amish romance novels—or at least she didn't read them often. Occasionally her friend Liza loaned her one and then it would have been rude not to read them.

"You say *entrepreneur* as if it's a bad thing, and why don't you want anyone helping at your house?" Becca didn't believe in creeping up on a subject—best to toss it out there and catch the person you were interrogating off guard.

"I didn't say I didn't want help."

"You didn't jump at the offer, either. I noticed that you have a way of turning the conversation away from yourself."

Daniel smiled broadly for the first time since she'd known him. "Didn't realize you were watching me so closely."

"Don't flatter yourself. I'm not in the market…"

"And why is that?"

"None of your business."

"True enough, and it's none of your business why I'd rather rebuild my house by myself."

His voice was joking, but his eyes had taken on a decidedly serious squint.

"Fine by me." She turned to study her hens. "I suppose I should introduce you to the group. Princess is a golden comet. Buttercup and Egg-bert are both Rhode Island Reds, and the other four are Sussex."

"What? They don't have names?"

"Betty, Pearl, Henny and Doris."

Daniel stared at the ground a minute. When he finally looked up, she knew he was laughing at her...even though he wasn't making any sound. She could tell.

"Naming hens is a common practice. They need to feel cared for in order to lay the maximum number of eggs."

"How are things going with Carl?"

"You know good and well that things are going terribly with Carl. That's why he's still banished to our barn."

Did Daniel just flinch when she said the word *our*? Interesting.

"The new roof is *wunderbaar* by the way. I'll be able to spend a lot more time over there now that I don't have to worry about the rafters falling in on me."

That definitely irritated him. He'd crossed his arms and was frowning at something on the horizon.

She moved next to him, mirrored his position and asked in her sweetest voice,

"Why did you buy the worst farm in town?"

"I'm not sure it's the worst."

"Oh, it is, trust me. I'm thinking maybe you bought it because you didn't want anyone bothering you."

"I'm not saying that's true, but I will say if what I wanted was to be alone, then my farm is a great place for that, or at least it was the first twenty-four hours I lived there."

Instead of being insulted, Becca laughed. She'd definitely managed to poke under his defensive, though polite, layer. She barely had time to enjoy the moment, though. He quickly turned the tables on her.

"Why are you so intent on making money?"

"There's nothing wrong with making money." She raised her chin slightly and tried not to notice that his smile had returned.

"Most girls in your situation would try to marry up instead."

"Marry up?" Becca clinched her hands at her side and hoped that her temper didn't pop the *kapp* off the top of her head. "You're saying I should marry up? You're actually suggesting to me that I should marry for money?"

"Oh, come on. Don't look surprised. Girls do it all the time."

"And you're an expert on this?"

"I'm not blind. I've seen it happen often enough, and I'm not saying anything's wrong with it as long as both parties are honest about their intentions."

"You're saying that the way to improve my lot in life is to hook my buggy onto some rich Amish guy's horse."

"I might not have said it that colorfully, but if the *kapp* fits…"

A low growl escaped Becca's lips. She could actually feel her blood pressure rise. Her neck and jaw muscles had gone suddenly stiff as if they'd been locked in place.

Daniel was like most other Amish men she'd met. Why had she for a moment imagined he might be different? Because he was as poor as they were? Obviously, that wasn't enough to give him a fresh perspective on life. He thought the same as every other single guy she'd ever known.

She was tired of it.

She wasn't going to demurely accept being put in her place any longer. She tried to count to ten, made it to three, and then gave up.

It was time to give Daniel Glick a piece of her mind.

Chapter Three

Daniel stepped back when Becca stepped closer.

The midsize mutt that had been dogging her steps apparently sensed the tension between them. Spotting a butterfly that was making its way across the field, the dog took off in pursuit. Daniel didn't blame him.

Things were about to go from bad to worse.

Daniel was well acquainted with a woman's temper. His oldest *schweschder*, in particular, had something of a short fuse, which made them all laugh after she'd *gone off* on someone. Amish women were supposed to be patient and kind, and Angela was both of those things once she calmed down. Still, he had learned at a young age to get out of the way when she was riled. He saw the same look on Becca's face now.

The problem was that he'd reached the limit of his patience with Becca Schwartz.

She was angry?

He wasn't exactly in the best of moods, either, so bring it on—but from a distance. He took two steps away from the chicken coop.

Her voice dangerously low, she said, "We may be the poorest family in town—"

"I never said that."

"And we may not have a fancy new saddlebred horse—"

"What does my horse have to do with this?"

"But we take care of our own in the Schwartz family. We help one another. If my *bruder* needs a buggy and can't afford it, then I don't mind working a little extra harder to help him, and I don't need you telling me—"

"I think you misunderstood what I was trying to say."

Becca's face had taken on a decidedly red hue, her hands were slicing the air with each point she tried to make, and her gaze was jumping around as if she couldn't decide what she wanted to take down first—him or the chicken coop.

"I understood what you said just fine. You think every single woman is looking for a rich man. Ha! I guess the joke's on you, since you're as poor as we are."

"There's nothing wrong with being poor."

"But you know the funny thing? We're not really poor, because we have each other. You, on the other hand, are over there with your fancy horse and your decrepit house and you have no one. As far as I know, you're on the lookout for a wealthy Amish girl so *you* can marry up."

"I didn't move to Indiana to marry." Daniel felt his own temper rise, and he fought to tap it down. Becca didn't know what she was talking about. She didn't know a single thing about his situation. In fact, it was almost laughable, because everything she thought she knew about him was wrong. "I moved here to be alone, so if you'd just keep your nose out of my affairs..."

"Oh, my nose is in your affairs?"

"You're over at my place every day."

"In our half of the barn."

"I saw you feeding carrots to Constance. Feed your own horse and leave mine alone!"

Again the growl, but this time she clenched her hands at her side and stomped away. He waited five seconds, stared at the ground and heard his *mammi*'s voice. *Tackle the problem, not the person.*

The problem, he realized, was that it wasn't as easy to be a loner as he had thought it would be. Well-intentioned people kept invading his space. Worse, he understood that he'd hurt her with his careless comment. That hadn't been his intention, but it had plainly been the result.

He prayed for wisdom even as he hurried to catch up with his pretty neighbor.

"Becca, I'm sorry."

"I don't want to hear it."

"But I need to say it." He reached out and touched her arm, causing her to halt so suddenly that he practically ran into her. "Look…"

When she pivoted toward him, he stepped back and raised his hands in surrender. "It's none of my business that you have a business streak, or entrepreneurial spirit, or whatever you want to call it. It's also none of my business what you hope to accomplish."

When she didn't respond, he added somewhat lamely, "And I do think it's admirable that you want to help your *bruder* Clyde."

Her chin came up and her eyes locked on his, but still, she didn't speak. Daniel's mind scrambled to remember what else he'd said, what he still needed to apologize for.

"It's actually very considerate of you to bring carrots to Constance. I'm sorry for what I said earlier—about you having your nose in my affairs. That was unkind. What I meant was that I'm not ready to talk about my life or my past. I'm... I'm a private person, and I don't...well, I don't share easily."

The truth slipped past his planned generic apology. It caught him off guard, and apparently, Becca hadn't been expecting it, either, because some of the stiffness went out of her posture.

"I plan to keep using our half of the old barn, whether it bothers you or not."

"Of course. That's fine."

She crossed her arms and squinted at him, some of the fire returning to her eyes.

"What I mean is that you don't need my permission. It's your half of the barn."

Which sounded so utterly ridiculous that he couldn't help grinning. Becca rolled her eyes and reached for her *kapp* strings.

She took a deep breath, stared at the ground, and then finally met his gaze. "I'm sorry that I lost my temper."

"*Nein*. I provoked you—unintentionally, but still I should be more careful." They both started walking back toward the picnic tables. "It's none of my business who you plan to marry or why you would want to do so."

"I'm a tad sensitive about that subject."

"Understatement of the year." He thought he'd said those words to himself, but she slapped his arm, so he must have said them out loud.

They were still out of earshot of the group, so he stopped and waited for her to turn to face him. "I'll make you a deal. You stay out of my business, and I'll stay out of yours."

"Of course."

"Seriously?"

"No problem. My life is plenty busy without solving the enigma of Daniel Glick."

He might have believed her, but then she smiled, raised her eyebrows and sashayed off toward the dessert table. He realized with sudden clarity that it wasn't him she was interested in, it was the mystery living adjacent to their property. Amish life could be slow at times, and Becca Schwartz was a nice-looking woman in her twenties, still living on her parents' farm. No doubt her life needed some excitement.

The issue was that he had no intention of providing her a welcome distraction. He wanted peace and quiet and solitude. He'd purchased those things as much as he'd purchased a rickety barn and broken-down house.

The challenge would be to stay out of

her way and not lose his temper again. He should be able to do both of those things.

Becca had reached the dessert table and was talking to Abigail. She looked back over her shoulder at Daniel, smiled too sweetly and then continued talking to her *schweschder*. They both laughed and then walked toward the house.

He didn't know how he knew it, but whatever was happening between him and Becca was just beginning.

Staying out of her way wasn't going to be easy.

Becca couldn't have explained why Daniel had aggravated her so. She certainly wasn't willing to examine her feelings on the subject of marriage. Doing so tended to put her in a funk for days. So instead, she'd sidled up to her *schweschder*, smiled back at Daniel and pretended she had a plan.

She needed a plan for dealing with their new neighbor.

Regardless of whatever his personal issues were—and he apparently did have issues that he was in no way going to talk about—he'd read her completely wrong. She was not searching for a husband in order to alleviate her family's financial problems. If she was supposed to find true love, she would. God would drop it on her doorstep—or rather God would drop *him* on her doorstep. Or maybe put the guy next door.

Ha! That hadn't happened.

So instead of worrying over Daniel Glick, she proceeded as normal for the next week—attempting to tame Carl-the-bad-tempered-rooster, helping her *mamm* with household chores, and keeping her eyes open for any new projects that might raise money for her family. Everyone called them her "get-less-poor" schemes, since a "get-rich" scheme seemed too far-fetched.

And while she did those things, she continued to try to learn more about their new neighbor.

On Friday, she decided she could use a few hours away from the farm, so she walked over to Liza Kauffmann's house to see if somehow she'd heard something that Becca hadn't. Liza had been her best friend for years and years. Liza understood her, though in many ways they were polar opposites. For one thing, Liza had plenty of beaus.

Liza was in the middle of making fresh bread. She punched the dough, turned it on the floured countertop and then proceeded to divide it in half. "I can't believe I haven't met him yet."

"How could you? He rarely leaves his farm."

She slipped the two halves into two loaf pans, covered them, then nodded toward the window. "Walk with me over to the shop?"

"Sure."

The fall day was glorious—leaves

crunched under their feet, and the sweater Becca was wearing provided just the right amount of warmth against the crisp autumn air. She'd be perfectly happy if only she wasn't so puzzled by Daniel Glick.

"Strange that he's not more interested in meeting some of the local girls."

"I guess."

"You would think that someone so... young..." Liza drawled.

"How do you know he's young?"

"Deborah told Mary, who mentioned it to me."

Becca somehow resisted the urge to slap her palm against her forehead. "The Shipshe grapevine is alive and well."

"Stop calling it that."

They walked into Liza's bakeshop, which was actually a small modular house that had been outfitted with shelves to hold the items she baked in their kitchen. Liza was an expert baker. Give her sugar, flour and any variety of ingredients, and she could create something that would make your mouth water.

She was two years younger than Becca, still enjoying the freedom of her *rumspringa*—which explained the cell phone and romance novels. Liza was also putting on at least ten pounds a year. None of those things mattered to the eligible men in their community. Liza could cook, and she had more interested males stopping by her place than she could shake a rolling pin at.

"I don't think you'd be interested in Daniel. He's older—older than us, and he's serious."

"How serious?"

"I've only seen him smile when he's teasing me about Carl-the-bad-tempered-rooster."

"Well, I'm not looking for a husband anyway."

"Still in no hurry to settle down?"

"Just because I love baking doesn't

mean I want to stay home every Saturday night."

Becca shrugged her shoulders at that comment. She was used to Liza's rebellious ways.

"I just keep wondering why Shipshe? Why that farm? What's he doing here?"

"I don't know, Becca. Life can lead you to strange places. I never thought I'd go to a Notre Dame football game, but there I was last weekend in a college stadium that holds eighty thousand fans."

"Did you wear your *kapp*?"

"I wore a cap, but it had a Notre Dame logo on it." Liza winked, then smoothed out her apron. "Don't give me that look. I wore blue jeans and a sweatshirt—it was all quite proper."

"But not Plain."

"*Nein*. It wasn't." Liza squirreled up her nose. "Don't you ever want to experience things? Other things?"

"Like what?"

"I don't know. The Notre Dame campus has Touchdown Jesus in the end zone, the Basilica of the Sacred Heart, and the Grotto of Our Lady of Lourdes."

"I have no idea what any of those things are."

"Beautiful, that's what they are. You know, Amish don't have a corner on all things to do with Christ. You'd be surprised when you step out of our community how much of *Gotte* is still around."

"Well, you don't have to lecture me about it."

"Guess I'm a bit touchy about it all. *Mamm* keeps trying to set me up with Amish men—respectable Amish men. She always makes sure I understand that they are the good, decent sort."

"I suppose I should be grateful my *mamm* is too busy with the twins to meddle in my social life."

"Take it from me—you really should be."

As she walked home, Becca couldn't help wondering whether Daniel would find Liza attractive. The man could use a wife, especially one that knew how to cook. Though the thought of Liza living in a house where the roof was falling in was enough to make Becca laugh out loud.

It was later that afternoon, while she was tending to her newest project, that she had a chance to tease Daniel.

He'd been avoiding her since Sunday dinner. It seemed he kept changing the time that he brought in Constance. She'd had little chance to properly pepper him with questions. So on Friday afternoon, she brought along a cookbook and sat down to page through it while she waited for him to bring Constance into the barn.

When he did, she pounced.

"Still not working on the house, huh?"

He didn't ask what she was doing on his side of the barn. In truth, you couldn't actually split a barn in half. They shared the large open area. Daniel kept Constance in one of the stalls on his side. Becca kept

Carl-the-bad-tempered-rooster and her other projects on her family's side.

"Still not working on it," he agreed.

"Aren't you worried about winter coming?"

"I'm more worried about the fields."

"Yes, I saw you out there working."

He didn't answer that. Daniel was good at not commenting on things, which made Becca want to provoke him all the more. Although *provoke* might be the wrong word. She was simply curious. Was that such a sin?

"Seems the girls in the district are all talking about you."

"Is that so?"

"You'll have a chance to meet them at church on Sunday."

Daniel grunted.

"My friend Liza, she's a very *gut* cook—baker mostly, but she can cook just about anything."

He walked to the other side of Constance to brush her down. That horse received more attention than the average Amish wife, Becca was sure of that.

"Are you trying to set me up, Becca?"

"*Nein.* I just thought you should know what you're walking into."

"Is that why you hang out over here? Trying to provide the Amish grapevine with new information?"

"That's what I call it, too."

"Every community has one."

"It's not like we have Facebook."

"What's that?"

"Or Twitter?"

"Twit who?"

"Or Snapchat."

Daniel placed the horse brush on a shelf and walked over to open the stall door, forcing her to back up. It was a half door, so Constance could stick her head out whenever she wanted. She imagined that he spent his nights sitting outside the door, singing to the spoiled mare. As he walked out of the stall and carefully secured the door latch, he asked in a low voice, "Are you sure you're Amish?"

"Pretty sure. If not, I have a terrible sense of fashion."

"What's wrong with your fashion?"

"Look at me. Long dress, apron, *kapp* on my head."

"Would you rather be wearing *Englisch* clothes?"

"Of course not. Why are we even talking about my clothes? Let's talk about you."

"Still nosing around."

"It's natural to share. I'll start. I'm twenty-four, I'm the second oldest of nine siblings…"

"I already know all of that." Daniel crossed his arms and leaned against the closed stall door. "Have you ever dated?"

"That's a rude question."

"I thought it was natural to share."

"Except I don't want to share about that."

"All right. Tell me about your projects.

What have you been doing on your side of the barn?"

"What?"

Daniel's smile brightened. He tucked his thumbs under his suspenders—which should have looked stupid, but actually made him look less stiff and more likable—and began to walk toward her side of the barn.

"Where are you going?"

"I should probably be aware of what's going on under the roof of my barn."

"*Our* barn. Remember? We both own it."

"Your *dat* and *mamm* own it. I'm sure they'd want me to keep an eye out."

"Hang on. That's none of your…"

But Daniel had already walked into the stall where she'd set up her latest project. It was closest to the outer door on her side and allowed in plenty of light so the plants could grow.

"What is this?"

"It's nothing."

He stooped closer to study the plants that were now six inches high. "What are you growing?"

"It's just a project. I received it through a mail-order service a couple of weeks ago, and I've been...you know...watering, making sure they have plenty of light, using these growing supplements they gave me."

When he turned toward her, she expected to see him laughing at her. Instead, his eyes had widened, and he was looking at her as if he'd just seen Carl dance a jig. He was looking at her with obvious disbelief.

"Do you know what this is?"

"Of course, it's..." Becca picked up the pamphlet that had come with the plants and peered at it. "From the family Cannabaceae."

"Cannabaceae?"

"I don't really know how to pronounce the word. Besides, it doesn't matter what it is. I take care of and grow the plants, then call this number and someone will come out to pick them up and pay me. It's a great deal. I can make five to six dollars a plant, which is a lot of money even if only two thirds of the plants survive."

"Becca, this is hemp."

"What?"

"It's hemp. Basically it's marijuana without the THC content."

"It is not. I wouldn't grow marijuana in my parents' barn."

"It's not marijuana. It's hemp. Did you apply for a license to grow this?"

Becca couldn't resist. Both hands planted firmly on her hips, she stomped her foot. "Read my lips. That's not what this is. It's just…it's just…"

She picked up the brochure again. "Some kind of medicinal herb." She'd meant to read the entire description, but then something had distracted her. Now she was having trouble focusing on the words. Various phrases popped out, like *industrial hemp, may contain a maximum*

THC content of 0.30% and *how to deal with thieves*.

Her chest started to tighten, sweat trickled down the back of her neck, and she felt a sudden light-headedness. The words on the brochure seemed to swim before her eyes, and when she glanced up, Daniel looked as if he was standing at a slant.

Daniel grabbed both of her hands and pulled her outside, into the fading light of a bright October afternoon. "Sit there. Head between your knees."

"Why?"

"You looked as if you were about to faint."

"I'm not the fainting type."

"So you might not recognize the symptoms."

"I might have made a mistake," she mumbled.

"What?"

"I said..." But when she raised her head, he was smiling at her, and she knew that he'd understood her perfectly well.

"It's not a problem," he said. "Just throw the plants away."

"Throw them away?" That idea brought the blood rushing to her cheeks. She sat up straighter, then rested her head back against the barn. "I can't throw them away. What if someone finds them?"

"No one will find them."

"Maybe Hannah and Isabelle."

"Why would they be out here in the barn?"

"They could get high."

"No one's going to get high. It's not marijuana per se. Did you even read the pamphlets?"

"I could burn them, but then we might all get high. Imagine Carl-the-bad-tempered-rooster high." She covered her face with her hands.

Daniel moved to sit beside her on the bench. "It's all a mistake. It's just a mistake. You can fix this."

"But it is illegal?"

"*Ya.* I suppose it is since you need a license to grow hemp here in Indiana."

"So I'll get a license."

"They're backed up. It's a nine-month process."

"Nine months?" She stood and began pacing in front of him. "What was I thinking? Why didn't I read the fine print?"

"Actually it says right here on the cover that you should check your state laws before growing."

Becca snatched the pamphlet from his hands.

"How do you know so much about this? Is that what you came here for? To grow hemp?"

"I'm not the one growing it." Instead of looking defensive, he still seemed to be holding in a belly laugh.

"But you know a lot about the subject. Explain that to me."

Daniel sighed heavily, then admitted, "Both of my *bruders* applied to grow it in Pennsylvania. You're right. It's a *gut* crop, and people use it for all sorts of things that are natural. It fits right in with our Amish way of life."

"What kind of things?"

"Clothing, rope, medicinal herbs and lotions."

"But I need a license."

"*Ya.* You do."

Becca crossed her arms, drummed her fingers and tried to think. She didn't have a license. Her parents couldn't afford any sort of fine. She surely didn't want to give what little money she'd saved to the Shipshewana judicial court. With one last look at Daniel, she turned and hurried back into her hemp room.

"What are you doing?"

"I'm taking these in to the police station." She began pulling the plants out by their roots and stuffing them into a box. Stupid plants. She'd done the math. She would have made at least five hundred dollars.

"You're taking that box in to the police station?"

"Sure. I'll just explain it's all a big mistake, and ask them to dispose of these for me."

"How are you going to get there?"

That stopped her in her tracks. How was she going to get there? *Dat* had their only buggy and had gone to visit his *bruder*. She couldn't ride her bike carrying the box she was holding, and she wouldn't be able to put them all into the one box anyway.

She expected to look up and see Daniel laughing at her.

She wouldn't have been surprised to receive a lecture from him, as he seemed to delight in her projects that went awry—at least he'd laughed a good deal over Carl-the-bad-tempered-rooster. But instead of haughtiness, she saw sympathy in his eyes.

Or maybe it was pity.

The one thing Becca didn't want from anyone was pity.

The expression was gone as quickly as it had appeared. Daniel stepped closer, reached forward and tucked a wayward lock of hair into her *kapp*. His touch caused a cascade of goose bumps to parade down her arms.

Why was he looking at her that way?

Was he laughing at her on the inside?

Did he see her as some sort of entertainment factor for folks stuck on a farm?

If she'd doubted Daniel's motives, his next words swept away any questions she might have had. "I'll harness Constance. We'll go together."

Chapter Four

Daniel was sorely tempted to laugh, but one glance at Becca convinced him to hold that in check. She had been completely silent for the entire drive. As he directed Constance to turn into the parking area of the Shipshewana Police Department, Becca finally broke her silence.

"I've never been to the police department."

"It's *gut* to do something new every day."

"This from the man who doesn't leave his farm."

"What are you afraid might happen?"

"They could arrest me!"

"Doubtful. I imagine they save their cells for unsavory characters."

"They could issue me a citation."

Daniel ran a hand over the right side of his face. He'd had a few encounters with the police in Pennsylvania, mostly due to his two *bruders* acting out. On both of those instances, the police had been nothing but professional, but he didn't want to go into that story right now.

"I think you're going to be fine."

"How do I explain this to them?"

"I don't know. Start with the truth?"

She nodded as if that made sense, grabbed one of the boxes of hemp plants and took off toward the front door. Daniel grabbed the additional two boxes they'd needed and jogged to catch up with her.

The officer at the front desk had dark black hair pulled back in a braid, light brown skin and a name tag that read Raquel Sanchez.

Becca juggled the box from her right arm to her left, tugged at her apron and then blurted out, "I'm here to turn in these hemp plants."

The officer cocked her head to the side. "That's a new one. Take a seat over there." She nodded toward a small waiting area.

They waited fifteen minutes. Twice Daniel tried to start a conversation. Both times Becca looked at him as if he'd spoken in a foreign language. Finally, he leaned closer and said, "Stop worrying. You're not a criminal."

"But...in this instance, I sort of am."

"*Nein*. You're a person who misunderstood the rules and is attempting to make that right."

His words eased some of the worry from her face, though not all of it. Fortunately, Officer Sanchez picked that moment to appear in front of them.

"Sorry about the wait. I was covering for JoAnn while she took a late lunch break. Come on back, and bring those boxes with you."

She led them into a back room that held

four desks. Three of them were covered with stacks of paper, manuals and old coffee cups. Sanchez must have guessed what Daniel was thinking, because she shrugged her shoulders, sat down with a sigh and motioned to the chairs across from her.

"My fellow officers are a mess. They make fun of me for keeping such a clean desktop." She leaned forward and lowered her voice. "They say it's the sign of a sick mind. I say at least I can find my keys at the end of the day."

Daniel immediately recognized her as a kindred spirit, or at least he didn't think she was the type of officer to slap the cuffs on them first and ask questions later. Becca still seemed a bit tense. She was jiggling her knees so that the plants threatened to fall out of the box, and her hands were clutching the sides of the box so tightly that the phrase *white-knuckling it* came to mind.

Officer Sanchez turned her attention to Becca. "Miss…"

"Schwartz. Becca Schwartz, and this is my neighbor, Daniel Glick."

"Pleased to meet you both. I'm Officer Sanchez, as I guess you noticed from the name tag. Why don't you set that box on my desk before you spill dirt everywhere? That would make Johnson real happy, to come in and see potting soil all over my desk. He'd never let me hear the end of it."

Becca placed the box on the desk, then nudged it toward the officer. Clutching her hands in her lap, she launched into her explanation. "I didn't know what they were. I should have known. I should have read the entire pamphlet, but I was trying to make some extra money so my little *bruder* could buy a buggy, and I didn't stop to consider the nature of what I was doing."

She pulled in a deep breath as if she was about to dive deep, and plunged back into her explanation. "Daniel is the one who noticed what kind of plants they were. He explained to me that I need a permit or certification or something, which I don't have. And I didn't know what to do. Didn't know if I should burn them or toss them or what. So I thought the best thing was simply to bring them to you and confess."

Sanchez waited, her eyebrows raised as if she was preparing herself for another deluge of words, but Becca was apparently finished explaining. She rubbed the palms of her hands across her apron, glanced at Daniel, then turned back toward the officer.

"Okay." Sanchez leaned forward, picked up a pen and used it to push around some of the leaves on the plant nearest her. "These are plainly hemp, not marijuana, and it's true you do need a license to grow a hemp crop. Once you realized your mistake, you could have destroyed the plants—"

"I was afraid my rooster would get into them if I simply tossed them into the compost pile, or my little *schweschdern* might find them. I was afraid it would make them sick or even…even high."

"Nope. Hemp can't do that."

Becca had tucked the pamphlet into her box, and Sanchez reached for it, pausing to ask, "May I?"

"*Ya.* Of course."

She perused it for a minute. "Interesting. It sounds to me like instead of applying for their own permit, this company is depending on small independent growers to do their work for them. Saves them money and paperwork. Do you mind if I keep this?"

"Not at all."

Sanchez turned to Daniel. "Sir, you can place those two boxes over there, against the wall. I'll see that these are properly disposed of. Thank you for bringing them in."

"That's it?" Becca hopped to her feet as soon as Sanchez stood. "You're not going to interrogate us or cuff us or read us our rights?"

If Daniel wasn't mistaken, a smile twitched at the corner of Sanchez's mouth, but she managed to maintain a thoughtful look as if she were seriously considering doing any of those things. Finally she shook her head and said, "I don't think that will be necessary seeing as how you made us aware of the situation and brought in the plants. You did bring in all of the plants?"

"Oh, *ya*. These three boxes, they're all I purchased. Of course they were only seeds when they arrived in the mail, but I've been tending to them every day and they grow quite fast. They were supposed to fetch $6 a plant, but I guess that's money I'll never see."

"You might consider reporting your experience to the Better Business Bureau, and I'll turn this pamphlet over to my supervisor."

She walked them back to the front of the

station. When they stepped out into the waning sunlight of a beautiful fall day, Becca pulled in a deep breath.

"Seems like we were in there forever."

Daniel glanced at his watch. "Less than thirty minutes."

"Longest thirty minutes of my life."

"Were you really worried?" He put his hand in the crook of her elbow and guided her toward the buggy.

"Worried? I kept thinking that my *mamm* would have to deal with my siblings all by herself, and that we couldn't afford a lawyer even if we knew one, and that I wouldn't look *gut* in a prison jumpsuit."

Daniel couldn't help laughing at her last point. "*Ya.* Prison jumpsuits definitely aren't Plain."

By the time he'd unhitched Constance from the post and hopped up into the buggy, Becca was leaning forward, arms crossed and resting on her knees, head bowed and face hidden in her arms.

"It's not that bad."

"Oh, but it is."

"You're being too hard on yourself."

"I wasted fifty dollars on those plants." She sat up and glared at him, as if he'd been the one to suggest she buy them in the first place. "Do you realize how much fifty dollars is?"

"*Ya*, I think I do."

"It's a lot of eggs, I'll tell you that. Quite a few of them, since I only charge $3.50 for a dozen. Let's see…that's…let me see how many eggs that is." She wrinkled her brow as she tried to do the math.

"Around one hundred and sixty-eight."

"How did you figure that so fast?"

"Simple math. It's a lot of eggs."

"Obviously."

"I think you need some ice cream."

"I can't afford ice cream!" She positioned herself in the corner of the buggy, studying him as if he'd lost his mind.

"My treat." Before she could say another word, he turned toward Howie's.

It wasn't until they were settled at a picnic table with cups of ice cream in front of them—strawberry for Becca and chocolate for him—that she seemed to pull herself out of her funk.

"I'll think of something. This is a setback, for sure and certain it is, but it's not the end. *Gotte* probably has something better in mind. I need to keep the faith, not give up. I need to move on and leave what's done—including those hemp plants—in the past." She was accentuating each phrase with her spoon and a good amount of strawberry ice cream had dripped across the table.

Daniel snagged one of their napkins and wiped it up before she stuck her sleeve in the mess.

"Danki."

"Gem Gschehne."

"You must think I'm crazy."

"Not at all. It's only that…well, never mind."

But he'd already stepped his foot in it. No way Becca was going to let him back out.

"Only what?" She stuck her spoon into her half-filled ice cream cup and crossed her arms. "Only what? You might as well say it. Whatever it is, you've got it written all over your face."

"I do?"

"*Ya.* Tell me how I'm wrong."

He actually thought she was adorable, but he wasn't about to say that. Whoever married Becca Schwartz would never suffer from boredom or monotony.

"You said that *Gotte* probably has something better in mind for you, but it seems to me that *Gotte* isn't a wishing well. I don't think faith works like that."

"What?" Now Becca dipped her chin and gave him a look that suggested trouble was coming. "Did I say that *Gotte* was a wishing well?"

"*Nein,* but the way you were talking, like if you do the right thing, pray the right prayer, have the right attitude, then the answer would pop up. I'm not sure that's what the Bible promises."

He thought she would argue, but instead, she stared at her ice cream, picked up the spoon and took another tenuous bite.

"I didn't mean to criticize."

"No, you're right. I try to be upbeat and optimistic, but most of the time I have no idea what I'm doing. I want to help my family. Surely I can. If I just hit on the right idea, I could improve our situation. And I believe that *Gotte* wants that. He wants what is best for my family—"

"He's already given your family what they need, Becca."

"And what is that?"

"Each other."

The setting sun cast a long shadow across the fields as they made their way home. The ice cream had made Becca sleepy—that and the emotional highs and lows of the last few hours.

Realizing her plants were illegal.

Agonizing over what to do with them.

Deciding to go to the police.

Daniel insisting on going with her.

The understanding police officer.

And beyond all of that, Daniel's assertion that *Gotte* had given her family what they need.

"Why are we so poor?" she asked, darting her glance his way, then back out toward the October evening.

"I'm not sure what you're asking."

"If *Gotte* has given us what we need, why are we so poor?"

"Are you?"

"You know we are. We are. You are. The neighbors around us are. We definitely don't live in the affluent part of Shipshewana."

"Who decides what it even means to be affluent?"

"Oh, come on." She again cornered herself in the buggy and scrutinized him in the waning light. "Affluent. You're familiar with the word. It would mean that there's a *gut* layer of top soil on your farm, and that you don't have to try to fit ten people into one buggy, and that you would have a home with an adequate roof on it. That kind of affluent."

Instead of being offended, he laughed. Becca was learning that underneath his gruff exterior, Daniel Glick had a sunny disposition. Who would have guessed?

"I suppose my point is that we're not hungry and we're not alone. Your family, they have their health and they have each other."

"You're alone."

Daniel waved that away. He didn't even attempt to address it. "Your community is a *gut* one. I've only met a few people so far, but no one seems to look down on anyone else. They seem helpful. As you have pointed out on more than one occasion, plenty of people have offered to help me."

"And yet you turned them down. Care

to explain that? Because I still don't understand."

"I don't think I owe you an explanation, Becca."

"Well, Daniel. I didn't say you owed me one. I was asking a simple question, a neighborly question. You were just pointing out the value of having helpful neighbors and family around, and yet you're all alone. What is that about?"

"It's not about anything." He frowned at Constance, something Becca had never seen him do before.

"Why are you living alone?"

"Again, none of your business." He pushed his hat farther down on his head, nearly covering his eyes, which had taken on a decidedly hostile glint.

"And how did you afford this horse?"

"That again?"

"Yes, that again. What are you hiding, Daniel? Or what are you hiding from?"

He glanced skyward, as if petitioning the Lord for answers. He pulled in a deep breath and finally glanced her way. "I was only saying that perhaps you don't need to feel so anxious. *Gotte* is still in control. We can rest in that knowledge."

Which had such a ring of truth to it that Becca felt a tad guilty about prodding him for information. "When you explain it that way, I suppose you're right. We do have much to be thankful for. It's only that life is so hard."

"Maybe it's supposed to be."

"Hard?"

"Uh-huh."

"That's a depressing thought."

Daniel laughed as he directed Constance off the main road. "Growing up, my *dat* used to ask me this question. *Is life a joy to be lived or a problem to be solved?*"

"I'll take joy."

"*Ya*, that was my answer, too, but the older I get, the more I understand that there are many problems to be solved or at least trials to be endured. The real question is whether we can maintain a joyful attitude during the process."

He guided Constance down her lane and pulled to a stop in front of the house.

"You could have driven on to the barn— *our* barn."

"I figured you might have done enough problem-solving for one day. You didn't need to face Carl-the-bad-tempered-rooster after the last few hours you've been through."

At that exact moment, the animal in question dashed across the yard, crowing and flapping his wings as he chased one of the barn kittens. Hot on Carl's tail was Cola, beagle ears bouncing, tail pointed high, eyes locked in on the rooster.

Becca placed a hand over her mouth, afraid that if she started laughing, she'd never stop. She hopped out of the buggy, waved goodbye and dashed up the steps. As he drove away, her mind replayed his words. *There are many problems to be solved or at least trials to be endured. The real question is whether we can maintain a joyful attitude.* She couldn't help wondering how Daniel could be so wise at such a young age.

Or at least he seemed wise to her.

He certainly wasn't dashing around starting new projects every week. No, Daniel's method was slow and steady, and she could probably stand to learn from that.

Though there was something about him, some mystery, that he was holding close, and she meant to solve it.

She walked into the kitchen as dinner was being served. Her *mamm* smiled and her *dat* nodded, and her little *schweschdern* scooted over to allow her a place on the bench.

They all bowed their heads and silently thanked the Lord for the food. And in that moment, Becca meant it. She didn't much care that once again they were having soup and sandwiches. She was thinking about what Daniel had said, that they really did have all they needed.

She couldn't hold on to it, though.

The peace and contentment slipped away like water you tried to cup in your hand. Her *bruder* Clyde was talking about a buggy he'd seen in town. "Needs some work, but I could get it real cheap."

David was explaining how he'd once again patched the tire on his old bike. The thing was more patches than original tire at this point.

Georgia was squinting at the book she was hiding in her lap. Probably she needed new glasses again.

Before dessert was done, Becca was once more flipping through ideas in her mind—there really were endless opportunities to earn money to help her family. It was all good and fine for Daniel to be happy in his poverty. He had no one to worry about except himself. She had a family, and she meant to find a way to help them.

As for Daniel Glick, he'd managed to distract her with his talk of contentment and *Gotte*'s provision, but if he were as content as he claimed, wouldn't he be more willing to share about his past?

What was he hiding?

What was he running from?

Daniel was a likable guy, and he'd certainly helped her out of a tight spot, but there was still a mystery there. Mysteries bothered Becca. They were like novels with the final chapter missing. Something deep inside her worried a thing until it came to a satisfactory conclusion—good or bad.

She simply couldn't abide leaving matters unresolved.

She'd figure out the details of Daniel's past. The question was whether she'd still think he was a *gut* neighbor, a *gut* friend, once she did.

Becca woke the next day with a renewed zeal to learn the details of Daniel's life. He was their neighbor. Shouldn't they know what their neighbor was up to? Didn't the Bible say they were to love their neighbor? You couldn't love someone that you knew nothing about.

Since it was Saturday, she spent the morning helping with the baking and cooking. It wasn't until after lunch that she had a spare moment to herself. She walked outside and caught her *bruder* Eli standing in the backyard, practicing his baseball swing. "Don't you have chores to do?"

"I finished mine."

He swung the bat again, watched the imaginary ball fly into imaginary bleachers. Eli was tall and thin and talented with a baseball. It was rare that he wasn't carrying around a baseball bat or rubbing oil into his baseball glove. He was in his last year of school, and Becca almost envied him that final year of childhood. Soon enough adults would be asking him what he meant to do with his life, and when he was going to join the church, and who he was going to marry.

"Say, I could use your help with something."

Again he swung the bat, following through and smiling that he'd no doubt hit another home run.

"Eli, are you listening?"

He slowly turned toward her and seemed to come back to Earth. "*Ya*. Sure. Of course I am."

"*Gut*. Here's my plan."

Fifteen minutes later, Becca and Eli had crossed their property, walked through the old barn and popped out the other side.

"You sure we won't get in trouble for this?"

"For what?"

"Snooping in someone else's house."

"I'm not going in his house. I'd never do that. I'm simply going to look around his back porch."

"Isn't that snooping?"

"Don't you want to know what's going on with our neighbor?"

Eli shrugged and tossed his baseball in the air, catching it as if it were a yo-yo attached to a string. "Daniel seems like a nice guy to me. The other day he told me that I have good follow-through on my swing."

Becca forced herself to pull in a calming breath. "Not the point."

They'd stopped near a small crop of fir trees. "He's over there in that field, picking up rocks for all the good it will do him. Go over there and start a conversation."

"What am I supposed to talk about?"

"Rocks."

"I don't care about rocks."

"The weather, then."

Eli stared up at the clear blue sky, then looked at her as if she'd lost her mind.

"Why would I care about the weather?"

"Baseball, then."

He blinked twice. "Oh, *ya*. He used to

live in Pennsylvania. Maybe he's been to a Phillies game." Suddenly embracing his mission, he hurried away.

Becca waited until they looked to be deep in conversation. Then she slipped around to the back of the house. Mounting the back porch steps, she glanced around, then walked up to a window, cupped her hands and stared inside.

The interior of Daniel's house was worse than she had imagined. He must have begun pulling out rotten floorboards because there were holes throughout. The kitchen sink had been removed as well, as had the gas refrigerator and the lower cabinet doors. Peering closer, she noticed sunlight piercing down through the roof. That explained a lot. How long had the house been this way, with rain and snow falling down into the rooms?

What a mess.

She couldn't imagine living here.

She couldn't imagine why Daniel would want to live here, and that thought reminded her that she didn't have much time. She turned her attention toward the back porch. A sleeping bag had been placed near one wall. Next to it was an old crate with a battery lantern on it, and next to that was a camping cook stove. A few pots and pans were stacked neatly in a box, and his foodstuff was stored off the floor, stacked in another crate.

Wow.

Just—wow.

The nights were chilly now. Hadn't last night dipped into the thirties? And Daniel was sleeping on the back porch? Even if his sleeping bag was made for cooler weather, that couldn't be comfortable.

She stepped closer, nudged the sleeping bag with her foot and uncovered a journal.

Surely it wouldn't hurt to take a peek.

She glanced over her shoulder, confirming that no one was coming.

It wasn't snooping, not really. After all, the book had practically been sitting in plain sight.

She snatched it off the ground, ran her fingers over the plain cover, then opened it to the first page. His penmanship was surprisingly good.

Daniel Glick.

Lancaster, Pennsylvania.

Shipshewana, Indiana.

She walked to the corner of the porch and peered back in the direction of the field, but she didn't see anyone. No doubt Eli had talked Daniel into a game of catch.

She looked down at the journal, then turned the first page.

He who has no money is poor; he who has nothing but money is even poorer.

You are only poor when you want more than you have.

Penny-wise, pound-foolish.

Old proverbs, mostly related to money, filled the first few pages. There were also Scripture verses meticulously copied down.

Do not fear, for I am with you.

I know the plans I have for you.

When you pass through the waters, I will be with you.

Honor your father and mother.

Next to that last one was a question mark.

Interspersed between the proverbs and Bible verses were observations.

A beautiful sunrise can soothe the soul.

God's majesty is everywhere.

When a person's loyalty is divided, they cannot find happiness.

Hard work heals the heart.

She read the last one again.

What kind of hard work? Farming? Or rebuilding a house? And what part of his heart needed healing? Had he been hurt so terribly before? She ran her fingertips across the line and was so focused on the words, on what might be behind the words, that her mind didn't register the sound of boots on the porch steps.

Daniel snatched the journal out of her hands. "What are you doing? Why are you looking through my things?"

She'd seen Daniel irritated before. She'd seen him frustrated and put-out and impatient, but she'd never seen him angry. Becca glanced past him to Eli, who was standing on the bottom step, hands raised in a don't-ask-me gesture.

Daniel stared down at the book in his hands, then glanced up and shook it at her. "You have no right to snoop through my things. I want you off my property, and I want you off now."

Chapter Five

Daniel understood that he needed to calm down. His pulse pounded at his temples and a red aura surrounded his vision. Becca's expression shifted from stunned to alarmed to defensive. He strode away from her, needing space, needing to calm his anger. Unfortunately, that put him staring at Eli—a young kid who had probably been manipulated by his sister, a young kid whose biggest worry was the next pickup baseball game.

"Were you in on this?"

Eli glanced at Becca.

"Don't look at her. Look at me. Were you in on this?"

"Maybe. Becca just said we needed to know what was really going on with you."

"Oh, did she?"

Becca stepped forward to defend herself, but Daniel stopped her with an outstretched hand held up like a traffic cop.

"Tell me about that."

Eli nervously tossed his baseball from one hand to the other. "Uh, nothing to tell really. She said it was all right because she wasn't going to go inside, she just wanted to look around and make sure you weren't dangerous."

Daniel couldn't resist; he turned toward Becca wearing what he hoped was a wolfish grin. "Dangerous."

She'd crossed her arms, and there might as well have been a cartoon bubble hanging over her head.

"Save it, Sherlock." He turned back to her younger brother. "Eli, will you give me a few minutes alone with your *schwe-schder*?"

"Uh..."

"I assure you I'm not dangerous. If you're worried, though, you're welcome to send one of your parents over here—"

"That won't be necessary." Becca pushed forward, not stopping until she reached the porch railing. "You go on home, Eli. I'll be right behind you."

"Are you sure?"

"I'm positive. Obviously, Daniel isn't dangerous. I was being *narrisch*. Probably just reading too many *Englisch* suspense novels."

"You read those?"

"Go on home. If *Mamm* asks, tell her I'll be there in a few minutes."

Eli shrugged. "Okay. *Gut* talking to you, Daniel. Maybe you can play ball with us after church service tomorrow. You have a *gut* arm."

"Sure thing. I'm looking forward to it."

He waited until Eli was well out of hearing range before turning to Becca. His heart rate had settled, but his anger hadn't exactly cooled. He didn't deserve to be treated this way, and he was going to stop her prying into his life. He was going to do so this afternoon. They would settle this matter for once and for all.

"Look, Daniel, I'm sorry."

"You are?"

"I stepped over a line. I had no right to read your journal."

"It's not a journal, but you're correct. You had no right."

"But you can't blame—"

"Actually, I can. I can blame you for snooping through my things and for disrespecting my privacy. If you want to argue about that, we need to take this to our bishop right now—either him or your parents."

"You don't have to tattle to my parents. I'm not a child."

"You're not? Because from where I'm

standing, you certainly are acting like one."

"That's not fair."

"It's completely fair. You send your *bruder* to distract me, and then you come into my home…"

"Porch. I walked up *on* to your porch, which is technically just an extension of your yard."

He closed his eyes and prayed for patience. "You came onto my porch, looking through my things—without my permission. You disrespected me, Becca. I've done nothing to deserve that."

"Is that right?"

"Yes. It is."

"Then why the secrecy?"

"Stop this."

"Why are you living on a porch?"

"That's none of your business."

"Why did you buy this house?" She stepped closer; the repentant girl who'd been caught snooping had disappeared and a woman with a glint in her eyes had taken her place. "What are you hiding from, Daniel? Are you running from the *Englisch* law? What happened in Pennsylvania? Why are you even here? And who and where is your family?"

It was the last question that punched the anger out of him. All he was left with was a deep exhaustion, the kind that turned your feet to lead and made walking a thing that seemed nearly impossible. So instead of walking away—which was what he desperately wanted to do— he sank onto the porch steps and looked out over his pitiful back field.

"I just wanted to be left alone."

"But why? If you're going to be living next to my family, next to my impressionable younger siblings, don't I have a right to know the answers to a few basic questions?"

He wanted to tell her then—tell her everything. Explain about the inheritance and the way it had torn his family apart. Describe the women who had wanted what was in his bank account. Confess how much he missed his home and his parents and his six siblings. Admit how lonely he was.

Instead, he stood and stared down at the journal before stuffing it under his arm. "*Nein.* You don't. And if I find you on my property again, I will turn you in to the authorities."

Without waiting for an answer, he turned and strode away from the house, because what he needed more than anything was to put distance between himself and Becca Schwartz.

Daniel would have given much to skip church the next day, but he understood what was expected of him. He was well aware that if he didn't attend, he'd be visited by the bishop, watched more closely by the deacons, and placed under increasing scrutiny. They didn't see it as intruding on his life. They saw it as their obligation to help along a *bruder* in the faith. After all, they were his church family.

Skipping church wasn't an option.

Best to clean up, show up and put on a smile.

Best to appear to be one of them, even though he realized he was the furthest thing from that. He was a man who didn't fit in anywhere.

Church was held at the bishop's, and the weather matched his mood. Dark clouds had rolled in, the temperatures had dropped, and a north wind had picked up.

He was used to cold weather.

He didn't mind rain.

He only wished he'd been able to fix the roof on his house before winter made its appearance, but the barn had been in worse shape than he'd thought. The fencing and fields had needed tending to. The list of things needing done immediately was simply too long.

It was what he'd wanted, though—to have to work hard, to depend on his skills rather than his bank account, to make his own way. *Gotte* had granted his wishes, and yes, that realization did remind him of his conversation with Becca. He didn't believe *Gotte* was a wishing well, but in this case...well, it seemed as if his heart's desire and *Gotte*'s will for his life had coincided. His prayers had been answered. He wouldn't taint that by complaining.

He filed into the barn, hoping he could slip into the last pew. Bishop Saul had other ideas. He insisted that Daniel stand with him, introducing him to each family as they passed through the doors.

Becca's father smiled amicably, even as Becca pretended to be busy adjusting her little *schweschder*'s *kapp*. It was quite obvious that Samuel had no idea what had transpired between his daughter and Daniel. In fact, everyone except Eli seemed oblivious, and even Eli seemed to have forgotten. That was the way of fourteen-year-olds. Today's worries took precedence over any of yesterday's troubles.

"Can't play ball in the rain," Eli muttered. "Sure hope the weather clears." He then trudged away from them to join his *freinden*.

Daniel made a point to select a bench well away from Becca. In fact, he sat closer to the front, where he wouldn't have to see her. He thought he heard her voice a time or two during the singing, but of course he didn't turn to look. It was none of his business if Becca had a beautiful soprano voice.

He had figured that the sermon would be on loving your neighbor. That was the last thing he wanted to hear. He wasn't sure that particular commandment applied to snooping, eligible young women, but he'd rather not be reminded of the whole situation.

Since he was a young child, whenever he felt the least bit guilty about something, it seemed the pastor's words focused on that thing.

One summer he'd desperately longed

for a bicycle like his friend's. It was all he could think of. He'd even stopped by the store in town to see how much it cost, though at that point they hadn't received their inheritance and had very little extra money.

The following Sunday the pastor had preached on *Thou shalt not covet.*

Another time he'd desperately wanted to be in the field, working at their harvest, rather than in church. The pastor had spoken on honoring the Sabbath.

It was a regular occurrence for the sermon to speak directly to him.

To his relief, the first sermon was not on the Golden Rule, but rather it focused on Lamentations—not one of Daniel's favorite books from the Old Testament. He remembered being assigned to read it as a teen and falling asleep every single time. Today the words pricked his heart. "It is of the Lord's mercies that we are not consumed, because His compassions fail not."

He deserved to be consumed. He was

living a lie, but how was he to tell the truth? Always his life seemed like a puzzle that couldn't be solved. Yet the words rang through his heart—*His compassions fail not.*

If he hoped the second sermon would bring some relief to his raw feelings, he was sorely disappointed. "Timothy reminds us that even when we have trouble believing, even when our faith fails, *Gotte* is faithful." Saul smiled out over his congregation.

"It's a *gut* thing, *ya*? It's a thing that pricks our hearts and eases the burden on our shoulders. Like when you unharness your horse, you ease his burden, so *Gotte* does for us…if we let Him. If we are willing to let Him carry that which troubles us."

Daniel stared at the floor.

Was that what he was doing? Trying to carry his own burdens? But it couldn't be as simple as Saul suggested. Could it?

Could he simply offer everything that

troubled him up to *Gotte*? And what of his past? He had no idea what to do with his hurts and, if he were honest, his sins. Could *Gotte* actually wipe them away?

He longed to start over here, to start fresh. How? What was he to do about Becca Schwartz, who insisted on digging into his past?

If the day had been mild and the sun shining, he might have been able to avoid Becca. With the rain pouring outside, it made for a cozy and intimate affair in the barn. After the service had ended and the meal had been eaten, the children took off toward the back of the barn—to play with kittens and enjoy games of hide-and-seek. Even Eli was smiling, though Daniel heard him say that he was too old for such games.

The older members had pulled their chairs into a circle and were enjoying the time of fellowship. Most of the *youngies* stood apart, laughing and standing in groups of three or four. Several of the girls were looking his way, and Daniel knew he needed to escape before they found their courage to approach him.

It was too early to leave without drawing attention, so he stepped out of the barn doors, following the roof overhang around to the south side where the structure blocked the wind. He'd pulled up the collar of his coat and was nurturing his brooding thoughts, so he didn't watch clearly where he was going and nearly bowled over Becca.

His hands shot out to steady her, and she clasped his arms—blushing and laughing and saying that she was sorry.

"I'm the one that ran into you."

"True, but I should have been paying closer attention."

He was still holding her arms, as if she might topple over at any minute. Plainly she wouldn't. He dropped his hands and stepped back. "I didn't think anyone else would be out here."

"Only us introverts."

"You're an introvert?" He laughed, perhaps a bit too harshly, because her chin came up and her eyes narrowed. "What I mean is, you seem quite outgoing to me."

"Oh, *ya*. I'm a real partier." She trudged over to an old rocking chair and sank into it, staring out at the rain. "Most of the people my age are already married up. The girls in there have little to worry about other than their next date. They seem younger than me."

"You have *freinden*."

"Oh, *ya*. I do. My closest friend is Liza Kauffmann, but she was surrounded by boys as soon as the luncheon broke up. She's not really interested in dating right now, but she's too polite to tell them that."

"Maybe you should have rescued her." Daniel perched on the other rocking chair. He wasn't sure he was staying, but at the same time, outside with Becca seemed preferable to inside with all the eligible girls staring at him. Not that he considered himself such a great catch. It was just the way things were, especially when someone was new in a community.

"*Nein*. Liza can take care of herself. Trust me."

Becca studied him so long that Daniel began to squirm.

"What?"

"I don't know. What?"

"I mean why are you staring at me that way?"

"Only trying to figure you out. I thought you'd do everything possible to avoid me today." Before he could answer that, she pushed on. "I have to admit I didn't pay much attention to the sermons. I was too busy dealing with my own guilt."

"Your guilt?"

She fiddled with the sleeve of her dress, which was a pretty autumn orange. Daniel waited, not sure he should interrupt.

Clearing her throat, she finally looked up. "What I did yesterday was wrong. I suppose I knew that as I was doing it, but I justified my actions by saying that I needed to know what type of person you are. Already my *bruders* are looking up to you—"

"They are?"

"And I worry about people who might be a bad influence on them."

"I'm a bad influence?"

"None of that justifies my actions. Snooping is wrong. I'm sorry." Now she met his gaze directly. "Really I am. I'm not that kind of person, and I promise that I will keep a proper distance in the future."

He was a bit stunned.

He hadn't expected a direct apology at all.

If anything, he'd regretted how harsh his words had been—when he wasn't still angry at what she'd done.

Perhaps it was time that he be honest with Becca. He didn't have to tell her everything, of course. He didn't need anyone in Shipshe knowing that he was an

Amish millionaire. The term still struck him as something out of a novel.

But he could tell her a little, enough to ease her worries about her *bruders*. Perhaps he could stop guarding his past so closely. Maybe he could trust that burden to the Lord.

Watching Daniel, Becca almost started laughing. His range of expressions reminded her of looking through the twins' kaleidoscope. Just like those colors and shapes shifted and blended and altered, it seemed that Daniel's emotions changed and merged and finally settled.

She decided it was best not to say anything.

Instead, she waited.

Finally, he tapped the arm of his rocking chair and sent her a tiny smile. "I apologize if I've come off as secretive."

They both knew that he had been just that, so she again opted for saying nothing. It wasn't natural for her. A whole backlog of words was building up in her throat.

"It's just that when you move to a new place you're not sure who you can trust—who might be a gossip or who might ridicule you. I don't care too much what others think, but I don't want to spend time correcting rumors that are false." He crossed his arms. "Living with other people is a mess."

"Oh, and living in the woods alone is easy?"

"How would I know? I haven't tried it."

He wiggled his eyebrows, and Becca laughed. This was a Daniel she could like. Gone was the brooding, angry man from yesterday. Not that she blamed him one bit for his brooding or his anger. She'd deserved every ounce of it.

Daniel's mood shifted again. She sensed it immediately, like a change in the wind. She didn't know him so very well. How was it that she was able to read him so easily?

"I don't want to go into my past, Becca. Not now. Maybe not ever. I honestly can't say if or when I'll feel able to do that."

"All right."

"But I can assure you that it's nothing nefarious. Whatever crazy ideas you've concocted in your brain about me, they're not true."

"You're sure?"

"Yes." He looked at her and sat back, relaxing for the first time since he'd nearly ran her over. "Try me. Give me your craziest idea about me—the most far-fetched thing that has crossed your mind."

"Okay. You're part of the federal witness protection program."

"Definitely not. I heard they put those people up in pretty nice places, and my farm doesn't really fit that scenario."

"All right. Running from the law?"

"I've never broken a law. So, no."

"Left a girl at the altar—heartbroken and confused?"

He only hesitated a millisecond, but it

was enough that Becca knew she'd hit a nerve. She cocked her head to the left and waited.

"There was a girl, back home in Pennsylvania. I broke it off well before our wedding day. Furthermore, she was not confused or brokenhearted. She knew very well why I ended our relationship."

"Hmm. Well, I'm sorry, then...for whatever heartache you've been through."

"Danki."

Becca stood and paced to the edge of the roof overhang. The rain continued to fall, but more softly now. The land looked to her as if it was drinking the water, storing the resource for spring, when all of nature would need it for new growth and rebirth. She'd always loved fall and winter—it seemed to her the time of year when everything rested and prepared for what was to come.

She turned toward Daniel. "What about your family? I don't mean to pry. Honestly, I don't, but you and I both know that

Amish are all about their family. It just seems so odd for you to show up here—alone."

"All right. That's a *gut* point."

"You don't owe me an answer, Daniel. I understand that now. You don't have to speak of this."

"*Nein.* I said I would answer your questions if I can, and that one I can." He joined her at the edge of the roof over-hang. Together they looked out at the day, and it seemed as if they could watch fall change to winter before their eyes.

She thought of Daniel's back porch—the sleeping bag and little cook stove.

She wondered how he would make it through the winter if he didn't accept any-one's help.

But she didn't say either of those things. Instead, she waited, and though Becca had been somewhat cold earlier, she sud-denly felt flushed. Perhaps she was com-ing down with something. She wouldn't be surprised to discover she had a fever.

Even her heart was beating faster than it normally did.

"I have two *bruders*, both younger. Benjamin is twenty and still at home. Joseph is twenty-four, and he has left the faith."

"I'm so sorry. Did he become Mennonite?"

"Actually, I don't think he's become anything yet. He's a bit lost. I tried speaking with him, tried writing him, but he isn't ready to hear anything I have to say. Not that I'm the best person to offer advice. I haven't figured this life out, either."

"What about your parents? Do they have any influence with him?"

"*Mamm* and *Dat* try, but they argue quite a bit." He sighed, stretched his neck to the left and right. "They seem to be having trouble finding their own way. I don't think they'll be much help to Joseph."

"That must be hard on you. My *dat* is always telling silly jokes, and he doesn't seem to care at all how poor we are, but he's been a solid example for us."

"You're fortunate to have a father like that."

"And my *mamm* loves him. They're... well, they're a sweet couple. I always wanted someone to look at me the way my *dat* looks at my *mamm*." She ran both hands around the back of her neck. Of all the scenarios she'd imagined Daniel to be in, a broken family wasn't one of them. "Do you have any *schweschdern*?"

"I do. I have four."

"Have they remained Amish?"

"They have, but..." He crossed his arms and leaned against a wooden column, turning toward her as if he needed to gauge her reaction. "Sometimes it seems as if you can remain a part of something, but not genuinely be fully committed to it anymore. Does that make sense?"

"When a person's loyalty is divided, they cannot find happiness."

To her surprise, Daniel laughed. "Yes, you have a *gut* memory."

"I shouldn't have read your journal."

"It's not a journal."

"Whatever it was—I shouldn't have snooped."

"The book you found—I just call it my notebook—it's very personal to me. It's a place where I jot down things that I think might be true."

"That's the very definition of a journal."

He nudged his shoulder against hers. "Journals are for girls where they write about their feelings and practice penning their new last name."

"Maybe in fifth grade!"

"Did you have a journal like that in fifth grade?"

Becca rolled her eyes. "Did you forget what a big family I have? A journal in my house would not be wise. Pages would be borrowed for tic-tac-toe games, or a homework assignment, or a letter to our kin in Ohio."

"I didn't know you have family in Ohio."

"Oh, *ya*. My *dat* has a lot of *bruders* there. Cousins everywhere."

Hannah and Isabelle picked that moment to dash around the corner of the building, chasing one another and shouting at the top of their voices. It felt like being bombarded by a whirlwind. They were there and then gone.

Becca didn't want the conversation with Daniel to end, but she was probably needed inside. "I should go and see to the snack for the young ones."

"I'll help."

"You will?"

"Nothing else to do, and I'm avoiding all of those girls who are staring at me like I'm a new bonnet they'd like to try on."

Becca smirked and said, "Well, you're not humble."

"It's not that I think I'm *Gotte*'s gift to Amish women. It's only that I'm new in town."

"No worries." She patted him clumsily

on the arm. "Someone newer than you will come along, and their attention will be diverted."

"One can hope."

They turned and began walking back toward the main room of the barn. Halfway there, Daniel tugged on her arm. She stopped, pivoted and looked up at him. Daniel Glick had a strong jawline and very attractive eyes.

Which didn't matter to her one bit.

Staring into someone's eyes was what a person did on a date, and she and Daniel were certainly not dating. In fact, dating was the furthest thing from her mind.

"So we have a truce?"

"Oh, *ya*. Now that I know you're not running from the law or anyone else."

"Excellent."

"Still don't know why you won't accept help on that ramshackle house."

"Still none of your business."

"You can't plan to sleep on the porch all winter."

"There's always the barn, which is in pretty *gut* shape."

"You and Constance can keep each other company."

"And Carl-the-bad-tempered-rooster."

"Never trust that bird. I wouldn't put it past him to peck you while you sleep."

"I'll make sure he's safely penned up before sleeping in the barn."

"Uh-huh. You don't know how clever he can be. I've yet to find a way to keep him in a pen."

And with that banter, their friendship— if that was what they wanted to call it— seemed to shift to solid ground. She could definitely do worse than having Daniel for a neighbor. It was better than a doting old couple. He'd come out of his funk eventually, meet some girl who caught his fancy, marry and have a passel of kids. She could watch it all happen from her side of the barn.

For some reason, that thought didn't please her nearly as much as it should have.

Chapter Six

Two weeks passed; October gave way to November, and the truce between Daniel and Becca held. She had stopped snooping, as far as he could tell. She seemed satisfied with the less-than-complete answers he'd given her.

The only answers he could give her.

Daniel understood that Becca was worried about protecting her family. Somewhere along the way, she'd designated herself as the mother hen, in spite of the fact that her mother, Sarah, seemed perfectly capable of handling anything that came along. It was a large family, though, and Daniel was slowly feeling closer to all of them. It was hard not to. Sort of like having a litter of Labrador puppies next door that constantly frolicked in front of you, asking to be noticed.

Not that he was comparing Becca's family to a litter of pups. Okay, he'd just done that very thing, but the comparison fit.

"Are you sure you want to do this today?" Becca's *bruder*, David, was staring at him quizzically.

"Finish this field and all the winter crops are in."

"*Ya*, but...you don't look like you feel so good."

Daniel used his sleeve to swipe beads of sweat from his forehead. "I'm fine."

"You're sweating."

"I always sweat while I'm working."

"It's forty-five degrees out here—tops. There's a north wind, and it's cloudy." David pulled up the collar on his coat. "I think you're coming down with something."

"And I think you're avoiding my south field." Daniel attempted a grin though it hurt his head to do so. "Or maybe you can't keep up with me."

"Dream on, old man."

They spent the next four hours planting a cereal rye cover crop. When they paused for a break, David peppered him with questions.

"You're not going to harvest this?"

"*Nein*. We till it under in the spring."

"Why plant it if you're only going to till it under?"

"Provides biomass, crowds out weeds, and deer will graze on it."

"You plan on hunting?" Now David was grinning. "We only have the one deer rifle, but we try to harvest a few deer each year."

"Most Amish do—it's free meat, and most families can use that."

"My family certainly can." David was unerringly good-natured. His family's financial situation didn't seem to bother him a bit. "*Dat*'s never planted a cover crop."

"When we're done here, we'll take the extra seed over to your *dat*. See if he'd like us to plant it."

"He's working at the RV plant this week. He doesn't like the hours, but we needed the money."

"All the more reason to share the extra seed. You and I can take care of the planting as long as he thinks it's a good idea. You can ask him tonight."

"Sounds like a plan."

But by that evening, Daniel knew that he wouldn't be planting in the Schwartz field the next day. His body hurt all over, and he couldn't eat the meager dinner he'd put together. Shivers racked his body, but sweat dripped from his face. He had definitely caught some sort of bug. Hopefully it was the twenty-four-hour variety.

His living arrangements probably didn't help. He'd taken to sleeping in the house as the temperatures had dropped, but there was no way to heat even one of the smaller rooms because the roof still needed so much work. Not to mention there were gaps around the window frames that he'd stuffed with newspapers.

"Next week," he croaked as he hunkered down in his sleeping bag. He should have started working the roof sooner, but the crops had taken precedence. The roof could wait. If he didn't plant the cover crops, next year's harvest would be half what it could be.

He fell into a troubled sleep, peppered with images of Constance looking through his house window, David sitting in the middle of his field pulling up plants by the roots, and Becca standing at the fence, jotting notes on a pad of paper that she stuck in her pocket. He tried to call out to each of them, but no one seemed to be able to hear him.

And then he was back in Pennsylvania, at his parents' home.

They were arguing about Joseph moving to town. His *bruder* was standing on the front porch, his arms crossed and his back to his family, and Daniel? Daniel was where he'd always been, standing in between them, trying to forge some type of peace.

He woke to a cool hand on his forehead and sunlight streaming through the window. Blinking to clear his vision, he took a moment to realize that Becca was popping in and out of his line of sight, and even longer to realize that she was speaking to him or at least about him.

"I don't know what you were thinking."

He attempted to sit up, but the room tilted. He fell back against the sleeping bag.

"Stubborn. That's what this is about, and maybe a lack of common sense. I'm really not sure which is the most dangerous."

He tried to reach out his hand, to stop

her as she moved away. The last thing he heard was her calling to someone.

"David, go and get *Mamm*. Bring *Dat*, too, if he's home. We're going to need help moving him, and bring the buggy."

He wanted to argue that he wasn't going anywhere, that there was work to do, that he needed to look in on Constance. The words wouldn't form. He tried to swallow and felt intense pain stab through his throat, and then he was falling into the darkness that threatened to consume him.

Daniel opened his eyes, blinked and realized it was once again dark and that he was no longer sleeping on the floor.

Then where was he?

He rolled onto his side. The room seemed to tilt, and someone was groaning. He was groaning. The weight on his chest felt impossibly heavy, and he couldn't stop shivering.

Becca turned on a lamp, placed another

blanket around him and murmured, "Try to rest."

He glanced up to see her face in the lamplight—concern, worry and maybe fear colored her features.

What was he doing in their home?

Why was she sitting next to him?

How late was it?

What day was it?

None of those questions made it to his lips. He slipped back into a deeper darkness.

"You found him yesterday?" The person speaking placed a hand on Daniel's shoulder and shook him gently. "Can you open your eyes, son?"

He did and flinched away from the bright light.

"One more time."

He didn't want to, but he did want this man to go away. He needed to sleep, needed to burrow down in the blankets and find some warmth.

"Now your throat."

Squeezing his eyes shut, he complied.

A tongue depressor was stuck in his mouth, and then someone swabbed his nose. He jerked his head away.

"I'm sure it is influenza. We have a particularly nasty strain going around this year. Everyone else in the house had their flu shots this year?"

"Ya." The voice was Becca's *mamm*'s, but it seemed to be coming to Daniel from across the pasture. "Bishop Saul is adamant about everyone having their vaccinations."

"Not all Plain people do. Tell Saul I appreciate his help." The man sighed and moved away from Daniel. "Here's a bottle of Tamiflu."

"We can't—"

"Pay for it? This one's on me. I'd suggest putting him in the hospital, but I suspect I know what your answer to that will be. Just follow the directions on the label, try to get fluids down him, and be sure to wash your hands after touching him or anything he's used."

"But the vaccinations..."

"They help, Sarah. An exposed person who has been vaccinated can still contract the flu, but they will have a lighter case. I'd rather there be no more cases coming from this household, so keep the kids at a distance and you and Becca wash your hands often."

Daniel wanted to open his eyes and see Becca.

He wanted to ask her to look after Constance.

He wanted to thank her for finding him, but he couldn't do any of those things. Maybe after he rested...

"He's coming around." Becca rinsed the washcloth in the basin of water and wrung it dry. When she placed it back on Daniel's head, his eyes popped open. "Welcome back, sleepyhead."

He attempted to struggle off the couch,

but Becca put a hand to his chest and gently pushed him back. When had she become so strong?

"Not so fast."

At that point, Sarah bustled into the room, followed by Hannah and Isabelle.

"Is he awake?"

"Can he play with us now?"

"Why does his hair look like that?"

Both girls flung themselves into a chair on the far side of the room, staring at their guest.

"We can't sit closer," Hannah explained.

"Cause you're sick."

"Bad sick."

"And we could catch it."

Daniel offered a small wave. Hannah and Isabelle giggled and waved back. Before Daniel could say anything, Sarah stuck a thermometer in his mouth.

"Hold your questions," she said, sitting down on the coffee table in front of the couch. "Dr. Neal said that if your temperature didn't break today, you had to go into the clinic, so we need to check this."

He raised his arm as if he intended to remove the thermometer, but Becca popped into his field of vision, shook her head and nodded toward her *mamm*. "You want to do what she says. *Mamm* isn't to be messed with when it comes to the flu."

Sarah smiled at him and tapped her foot against the floor. The girls' voices had dropped to a whisper, though Daniel was able to make out the words "horse" and "house" and "workers."

Finally Sarah took the thermometer from his mouth and held it up to the light from the window. "Only one hundred. Much better."

"Doesn't feel better." His voice came out resembling a bullfrog's, and he winced against the rawness in his throat.

"Hannah and Isabelle—I want you two cleaning up your rooms like I told you before. Becca, could you see that Daniel gets down at least a full cup of water? I'll go and heat up some chicken broth. I do believe you've turned the corner, Daniel." And then she patted his shoulder as if he'd done something praiseworthy.

The girls dashed from the room in a flurry of giggles and shouts.

Sarah picked up a tray and glided into the kitchen.

Becca took her place in front of him, perching on the coffee table. She held up a cup of water. "Want to give it a try?"

He nodded, though he couldn't take his eyes off her. Somehow the afternoon light had formed a halo around her head. Her lips were more pink than he remembered, and her freckles seemed to pop with the smile she wore. It was her eyes, though, that gave him pause—the look of concern caused a lump to form in his throat that had nothing to do with the flu.

He took a sip of the water, both their hands steadying the cup. He winced at the pain of swallowing and then drained the rest.

"I don't remember..." He tried to clear his throat, but Becca shook her head.

"You're only going to make it hurt more. Here, try one of these cough drops."

She unwrapped it and dropped it into his hand. He sucked on it for a few minutes while she watched him.

"I don't remember coming here, or... anything."

"What's the last thing you do remember?"

"Planting the cover crop with David."

"That was three days ago."

Becca almost laughed at the look of shock on his face, except it wasn't really funny. Nothing about the past three days had been funny. She'd been terrified when she'd found him burning with fever and unresponsive. She'd spent the last four days hovering and praying and trying not to worry.

"What happened?"

"You were supposed to bring the extra

seed over on Tuesday morning. When you didn't show, David went looking for you."

"And?"

"He could see you through the window, lying on the floor in your sleeping bag. He tried tapping on the window to wake you, shouting at you, but nothing worked. He didn't know what to do, so he came and got me."

"You told him to fetch your *mamm* and *dat*, and to bring the buggy."

"I did."

"You came into my house."

She dared him with a look. "I did not snoop this time. Obviously something was wrong. I wasn't going to let you just die there."

"Danki."

"Gem Gschehne."

Becca's *mamm* returned carrying the tray, which now held a steaming bowl of chicken broth and another cup of water.

"Becca, please help Daniel eat this— all of it. Also, it's time for another dose of his flu medicine." Sarah sat the tray on the coffee table next to Becca, smiled at them both and went back into the kitchen.

Becca wasn't sure if there was work in there, or if she was giving them time alone. Her *mamm* seemed to think there was something going on between them. Becca had tried to disabuse her of the idea, but it only made her *mamm* more convinced that she and Daniel were hiding their feelings for one another.

"I remember an old guy——" Daniel scrubbed a hand across his face. "He shone a light in my eyes and said for you all to stay away from me."

"Doc Neal. *Mamm* says he worries too much, but she did insist the girls keep their distance."

Becca picked up the soup bowl and the spoon. "Think you can handle this?"

"*Ya.* I can feed myself."

She didn't argue. Instead, she handed him the spoon and bowl, but his hand shook so badly that the soup sloshed right back into the bowl.

"Um. Maybe you could help me."

"I'd be happy to."

As he obediently swallowed each spoonful, she caught him up on what he'd missed the past four days. "*Dat* and David planted the extra seed in our back field. That was after they moved you here. Your temperature topped out at a hundred and five. Clyde and David went back to your place and fetched a few things—a couple changes of clothes, your hat and coat, and your journal."

"Notebook."

"Right, and in case you're wondering, I didn't so much as take a peek."

"I wasn't wondering." His eyes met hers and a shiver slipped down her spine. "That argument seems rather childish after... after this."

"Indeed." She cocked her head, so relieved to find that he was eating and talking that she felt a strong urge to give him a hard time for it all. "Quite impressive. I've never seen anyone with a temperature that high."

"I'm an overachiever."

"Apparently." She spooned more of the soup into his mouth, then offered him a napkin. He wiped his mouth, then sank back onto the pillow.

"Who turned this couch into a bed?"

"Oh, I did that—Francine and Georgia helped."

"How did your family get by with no sitting room?"

"That wasn't a problem. We just stayed in the kitchen, though honestly, if it weren't for you being contagious we could have danced a polka in here and you wouldn't have known."

"You know how to dance a polka?"

"Beside the point. You were out." She scooted the tray away, crossed her legs, propped her elbows on her knees and her chin in her hands. "Did you know that people talk a lot when they have a high temperature?"

"Uh-oh."

"Oh, *ya*. There was one name you called out over and over…"

David's eyes widened. "Who…"

"We tried to tell you she was fine, but you wouldn't be comforted." Becca would have liked to keep teasing him, but her *mamm* walked through carrying a stack of clean towels and popped into the middle of their conversation.

"Never heard a man go on so about a horse," Sarah said, smiling.

"Indeed." Becca wriggled her eyebrows. "She must be the love of your life, Daniel."

"She's okay?"

"She's fine," Sarah assured him. "David's gone over twice a day to see to her. You don't need to worry about Constance."

Her *mamm* walked back to the bathrooms, so Becca dared to lean forward and lower her voice. "You'd have been better off in the barn with that horse, than in that drafty old house. What were you thinking?"

He looked as if he was about to answer, but then another sound caught his attention.

"What was that?"

"What was what?"

"It sounded like...hammering."

"Oh, that. *Ya*. The community is rebuilding your house." Becca stood and began tidying the things on the coffee table, dropping the thermometer, cup of water and wet cloth onto the tray.

"Wait. What did you say? They're..."

"Rebuilding your house, Daniel. They've had prep crews here the last two days. The actual workdays are tomorrow and Saturday. It's a real shame that you won't be there. I guess you'll have to trust that they do the work the way you would have wanted it done."

"Wait. I didn't want..." He tried to sit

up, but he ended up grasping the back of the couch and taking deep breaths.

She almost felt sorry for him, but really, wasn't this his fault? If he hadn't been so secretive, if he'd accepted help when they'd first offered, he might not be in this mess.

Which wasn't quite true. He'd still have the flu. She knew it wasn't caused by sleeping in a drafty house. It was a virus that was caught from other people. They'd had half a dozen members at church come down with it. Daniel's case seemed to be the worst. That could've been because of his living conditions or the terrible state of his pantry.

He'd finally caught his breath, and reached for her arm. "They can't do that."

"They are."

"But I'll take care of it."

"You'll rebuild your house? Before the first snowfall? Did you forget that we're already in November?"

He flopped back onto his pillow and

closed his eyes, then threw his arm across his forehead. The expression on his face was pure agony. He was definitely being more dramatic than the situation called for. The Amish helped one another.

What was his problem?

Why was he embarrassed?

Was he actually too proud to accept help?

Or maybe he was feeling guilty that he hadn't taken care of his home before his fields.

She couldn't begin to imagine what was going on in Daniel Glick's mind, but she paused when he reached out and laid a hand on her arm. "I need to talk to the bishop."

"Okay. I'm sure he'll check on you tomorrow."

"*Nein*. I need to talk to him before tomorrow, before the real work begins. Can you…can you call him?"

"No need for that. I saw his buggy go by on the way to your place. I suppose he's there helping. If it's so important, I'll send Francine or Georgia over to fetch him."

Daniel closed his eyes and nodded.

He looked more than worried. He looked distraught, but the flu didn't seem to care about his new worries. The flu was still having its way with his body. By the time Becca had carried the tray to the kitchen door, she heard his soft snores behind her.

Her mind slipped easily back into its old track.

What was Daniel hiding?

Why the urgent need to talk to Saul?

And on top of those questions, a more pressing one: Why did she care so much about the concerns of Daniel Glick?

The sky was nearly dark by the time Bishop Saul walked into the Schwartz sitting room. Fortunately, the entire family seemed to be gathered in the kitchen. Daniel could hear their conversation and laughter and the general chaos that usually accompanied such a large household.

"Daniel, it's *gut* to see you awake."

Daniel pushed himself into a sitting position. He was suddenly aware that it had been several days since he showered, but that was trivial compared to what he was about to do.

"I need to speak with you…" He glanced toward the kitchen, knowing they couldn't hear what he was about to say, but worried that they might. "If now is a *gut* time."

"Now is an excellent time. There is no time better than the present to unburden your soul." Saul sank into the chair closest to the couch.

Daniel guessed his age to be near eighty. The man's face was a myriad of wrinkles that fanned out into gentle folds, and his neatly trimmed, white beard reached his chest. It was his eyes, though, that belied his calling in life—they were gentle, patient, kind.

"I haven't been honest about my past, and the work over at my house…well, I think it should stop."

Saul didn't argue, simply made a go-on gesture with his hand.

"I have perhaps misrepresented myself. That is to say, though I purchased a less than pristine property…"

"A bit of an understatement."

"I actually have quite a bit of resources."

Saul didn't answer, didn't react in any way.

A nauseous stomach now added to Daniel's other aches. He pushed the thought away. Nausea was the last of his troubles.

"What I'm trying to say is… I'm rich."

"I see."

"*Nein*. I don't think you understand. I'm a millionaire."

And then the story poured out of him. He explained about inheriting the money, how it had torn his family apart, how it had ruined his relationship with the woman he'd expected to marry. The sounds in the kitchen turned to cleaning dishes and homework questions and a game of chess, but that was all background to Daniel as he gave up the burdens of his heart to this man that he barely knew.

"I decided to move away, to live as if my life had never changed, to live as if I had nothing." He crossed then uncrossed his arms as he finally ran out of words.

Saul ran his fingers through his beard, tapped the arm of the chair and then sat forward—elbows on his knees, hands clasped together.

"It is not a sin to be wealthy, Daniel."

"It's not?"

"*Nein.* Remember the parable of the talents."

"I never understood that one."

Now Saul smiled. "*Gotte*'s word can be difficult. *Ya?* And at various times in our lives, it can speak to us differently. Go back and read the twenty-fifth chapter of Matthew, as you're recuperating. I think that you'll find comfort as well as instruction there."

"That's it? That's all you have to say? Read Matthew?"

"Paul is *gut*, too. In the first book of Timothy, he commands those who are rich to not be arrogant." Saul waited, a smile tugging at the corner of his lips. "Search your heart, Daniel. Have you been arrogant?"

"*Nein*. Stubborn, perhaps."

"Which we can deal with at a different time. Paul also says that the rich are to put their hope in *Gotte*, not in their wealth."

"My wealth has been nothing but trouble for me. *Gotte* has been—up until now at least—the only constant in my life."

"*Gut*. That's *gut*." Saul sat up straighter. "Paul goes on to say that the rich are to be generous. I suspect you have been generous with your resources, since you're certainly not spending them on yourself."

"But don't you see? People are going to show up tomorrow to work on my house. They're going to give of their time and use resources from the benevolence fund. That's not right. It's not fair. I could easily hire a contracting firm to come and do that. I wanted to live simply, to live without the money, but then this happened, and now I don't know how to fix it."

"It would seem to me that you've started down that path already, by talking to me. I will pray that you have wisdom in this matter, Daniel. We'll both pray that you know with certainty who you should share this with and when you should share it—if at all."

"But what about tomorrow?"

"What about it?"

"They're going to all show up to help, thinking that I'm poor."

"I'm not sure that's true. Our community would show up to help, regardless of your financial situation."

"Okay. Maybe you have a point." Daniel scratched at the stubble on his cheeks. He needed to shave. He needed to bathe, and his stomach was starting to grumble. But more than those things, he needed to settle this now. "But what about the cost?

The materials will be paid for out of the benevolence fund."

"That's not a problem. We often have anonymous donations. Search your heart, then donate what you can. If you'd rather not give it directly to Deacon Miller, I'll be happy to pass it along."

Saul stood, stepped closer and placed his hand gently on the top of Daniel's head. He prayed that Daniel would have wisdom and clarity in all things. What pierced Daniel's heart was when this man, who really knew very little about him, thanked *Gotte* for bringing Daniel to their community, for adding him to their numbers, and for turning him into a strong man of *Gotte*.

He wasn't sure those words described him.

But one thing he was certain of—he wished that they did.

Chapter Seven

Becca hadn't given up on the idea of earning extra money for her family. Clyde was still saving for his new buggy, but he also gave a portion of what he earned each week to his parents. He needed help. And Christmas was coming. Becca wanted Hannah and Isabelle to have something new. Georgia would love a new book, and she probably needed new glasses. Francine...she really had no idea what Francine would like. Apparently Francine had decided she was in her *rumspringa*, though she wasn't even done with school yet. If asked what she wanted for

Christmas, she'd probably say she'd like a new pair of blue jeans or to have her ears pierced.

Of course, gift giving wasn't the focus on the holiday, but still Becca dreamed of being able to surprise her family with a few nice things. She had a couple of new leads on earning a little extra money. Hopefully, during the next week, she'd have time to pursue them more.

Carl-the-bad-tempered-rooster wasn't exactly working out the way she had hoped. At least her hens had become used to his moody behavior. They no longer ran from him, but instead moved to the end of the chicken coop and watched him carefully. Sort of reminded Becca of the group of young women at church watching Daniel.

Oops.

How had that image popped into her mind? It wasn't exactly a kind one.

Which was beside the point. As she walked back from Daniel's house Sunday afternoon, a westerly wind pulled at her coat and nearly tugged the bonnet off her head. She only wore the black bonnet over her *kapp* in the worst of weather because it was old and not particularly flattering. She felt rather like a crow with it covering her head, but it did protect her from the wind, which was apt to change and come from the north any moment. November in northern Indiana was a tumultuous time.

Speaking of tumultuous, Daniel was standing on the front porch when she reached the house, and the look on his face reminded her of the stormy sky at her back—brooding.

"How do things look?"

"Aren't you supposed to be inside?"

"Is there anything left for me to do?"

"You mean besides running a farm? *Nein.* That's it."

"Good grief." He limped over to the porch swing and collapsed on it. "My entire farm is being renovated, and I can't even see it."

"You're getting stronger every day. Before you know it, you'll be healthy enough to escape."

"Now you're mocking me."

"A little."

"I suppose I deserve it."

"You do."

"I'm not ungrateful."

"Uh-huh."

"Seriously, I'm not. And your family..."

She sat down beside him on the swing because he once again had that faraway look in his eyes. She peered at him more closely. He looked rather lost. He'd always seemed to be a bit of an introvert, but since his illness, he seemed to drift off into his own thoughts even more often. Several times she'd walked into the living room to find him with his journal in his lap, a forgotten pen in his hand, and his gaze locked on something outside the window.

He had the ability to disappear right before her eyes.

She raised her hand and snapped her fingers to get his attention, then smiled when he looked at her as if he was surprised she was there.

"Where did you go?"

"I was thinking about your family."

"They're a lot. My family can be overwhelming, even to me, and I grew up with them."

"*Nein.* That's not what I meant."

He hesitated, and she thought he'd change the subject. That was usually what he did when she prodded. There was still something mysterious about Daniel Glick, and a small part of her remained determined to figure out what it was. She no longer thought he was nefarious, but there were other reasons that one went into hiding.

He shook his head and laughed, though there wasn't much happiness in it. "My family was big, but it wasn't like yours. We didn't play games together at night..."

"Is Eli bugging you about chess again?

None of us know how to play, so I suppose he sees you as fresh competition."

"No one wanted to read aloud a passage from the book they were reading..."

"Georgia will read to anyone who is sitting in one place for more than thirty seconds."

"And none of my *schweschdern* would have asked me what type of color she should dye her hair."

"She won't do it. I know Francine better than she knows herself. She was only teasing. At least I *hope* she was only teasing."

"The point is that my family wasn't close in that way. There were a lot of us, and sure, we sat around the dinner table together, but it wasn't the same."

"Oh." Suddenly she did understand what he meant, and she felt an almost overwhelming love for her big, loud, crazy family. Instead of sharing that, she wrapped her arms around her middle. "You seem anxious to go home."

"I can't believe they remodeled the entire house without me."

"Oh, *ya*. You won't recognize the place. There's a roof and everything."

"I'm strong enough to go home. Your *mamm* worries, but I think I'd be fine."

"And she would have agreed except that your temperature spiked again last night. Dr. Neal said forty-eight hours without a fever, and she's going to hold you to that."

"Maybe tomorrow."

"Maybe so." She cast a sideways look at him. "Off-Sundays are laid-back around here."

"I enjoyed the devotional."

"*Ya, Dat* has a real flair for making a passage in the Bible quite entertaining. He has a dramatic voice for reading." Her *dat* had read them the verses about Abram and his nephew Lot—how they'd disagreed and Abram had given Lot his choice of land. Lot had taken the best for himself, although it didn't end well for him. This was all before Abram had accepted *Gotte*'s calling on his life and become Abraham.

Becca wasn't sure how the story related to her and her siblings, although they did occasionally bicker over minor matters. Was that why her *dat* had picked it? Of course, after the Bible study and prayer, he'd snuck in a joke.

Who was the smartest man in the Bible? Abraham. He knew a Lot.

"It was nice to see your *Onkel* Jeremiah."

"He'll be gone most of December, visiting family in Ohio."

"And Abigail...she gets bigger every time she comes by."

Becca swatted his arm. "Better not tell her that. You'll have to hear her what-it's-like-to-be-pregnant stories."

"How about you sneak me out to the barn to see Constance?"

"I suppose I might be able to pretend that I need your help." They'd moved Constance to the closer barn, which made for easier feeding.

"Great." Daniel practically jumped off the swing. Just as she thought he probably was well enough to return home, he started a fit of coughing that lasted a good minute and a half. She wasn't glad that he was still ill. That was most certainly not the emotion she was feeling. But she also didn't want him to go home just to have a relapse. He'd scared a year off her life the first time. He owed it to her to be completely well before moving back into his own place.

"After we check the horses, *Mamm* should have dinner ready. It's usually just cold sandwiches on Sundays."

"Sounds *gut*."

"And I'm pretty sure there'll be a game of Pictionary after that."

"Never played it."

"You've never played Pictionary?"

"Nope."

"*Gut*. You should be easy to beat."

She bumped her shoulder against his as they walked back into the house. Twenty minutes later they were in the barn, brushing down Old Boy and Constance. Becca couldn't imagine who Daniel would ever let close enough to even have a relationship, let alone marry. Whoever the gal was, she'd need a lot of patience, because he absolutely adored that horse.

A girl who cared about him could get jealous over such a thing. Not that she would know anything about that.

It was actually Thursday before Daniel was able to go home. He did have a relapse—this time only running a low fever, but it was the cough that complicated things. It felt as if his ribs were bruised. He couldn't imagine trying to cook for himself or do his own laundry or even take care of his own horse.

That last one really rankled him.

He knew that Clyde and David and even

Eli were caring for the mare, but she was his responsibility.

As the week progressed, he slowly regained his strength.

Thursday morning, he'd showered, shaved and agreed to stay until lunch. Then he was going home—for good. He hadn't even seen the place since the workday. He was quite eager to look over what had been done. It couldn't all be finished, as Becca had suggested. Surely there would be work for him to do?

As he attempted to restore the sitting room to its pre-infirmary condition, he marveled that he'd been staying with the Schwartz family for ten days. Had he ever stayed in anyone's home that long? Come to think of it, he'd never stayed with anyone at all—except for his parents, of course.

The last ten days had offered his first insight into how other families lived, and as he'd confessed to Becca, it had helped him to realize that his own family was dysfunctional in more than one way—in more ways than just the wealth they'd inherited. He'd had two more visits with Saul, and the older man had been a great sounding board—only offering his opinion when Daniel flat out asked for it.

His most recent suggestion had been that Daniel write to his parents. Daniel wasn't sure he was ready to do that, but he was at least considering it. Saul's words reverberated in his mind at the strangest times.

Anger is a heavy burden for the one who carries it. Best to let it go.

Could it possibly be that easy? Could he just let it go? It wasn't as if he could tie his feelings to a balloon and watch them float away. Could he forgive his family for all the hurtful things they'd said to one another? He hadn't been completely innocent, either. There were things he needed to apologize for. He was already composing the letter in his mind, though he wasn't ready to commit it to paper.

Becca walked in the room and looked around in surprise.

"You're ready."

"Nearly."

"Lunch will be in a few minutes."

"*Gut*. I'm starved."

"Your appetite has definitely returned." She walked over to the bookcase and picked up his journal. She turned toward him, holding the journal in one hand and a duster in the other. She was a beautiful woman—golden blond hair peeked out from her *kapp*, freckles dotted her cheeks and nose, and her blue eyes were something a guy could get lost in.

At the moment she was pretending to be quite serious, but her eyes gave her away. Becca's eyes nearly always held laughter, in spite of her obsession to work her family out of their state of poverty.

"You don't want to forget this."

"*Danki.*"

"I know you've explained that it's just your thoughts and that it's not a journal."

She shook her head and laughter brightened her eyes. "But where do you find this stuff?"

The last few evenings he'd had trouble sleeping, so he'd sat at the kitchen table and written in it. The first time Becca had joined him, he'd immediately shut the book, but as he grew more comfortable around her he'd begun sharing snippets. When she hadn't mocked him, he'd shared more, so now he knew her question was in earnest.

"Some of it you just learn the hard way."

"Is that so?"

"*Ya*, you being so young, you probably can't imagine that."

"I keep forgetting you're an old man of thirty while I'm a young chick of twenty-four. Okay, learn it the hard way. What else?"

"Read. Some things you can learn from reading."

"The Bible."

"Sure, but other books, too. Men and

women have been sharing what they learned through writing for a very long time."

"Now you sound like Georgia." She ticked off his answers on her fingers. "Learn the hard way. Read about it. Are those my only options for finding wisdom?"

He stepped closer and breathed in the scent of her. For reasons he couldn't have explained, his ex-fiancée, Sheila, popped into his mind. He could remember how it felt to be hurt by her, but looking back now, it was as if those things had happened to someone else. He supposed he still bore the scars of her betrayal, but it no longer bothered him like it once had. "Heartbreak. I think you can learn from that."

She cocked her head and looked up at him. "Has your heart been broken, Daniel?"

"Yes. Once. I seem to have healed."

"Uh-huh. I think I'll pass on that one. Any other avenues of wisdom open to me?"

"Age, which we sort of already covered."

"You're telling me to get older?"

"Sure." He reached forward, tucked a

wayward lock into her *kapp* and allowed his hand to linger there. Her eyes widened, practically daring him to…to what?

Fortunately, her *mamm* called them to lunch then. Instead of turning and walking away, Becca tucked her hand into the crook of his arm. "Come on, old man. Maybe you can share your wisdom during our meal—entertain my *mamm* and *dat*."

Daniel barely heard what she was saying. He was focused on the feel of her hand on his arm, the closeness of her, the way that life seemed simple to Becca—family or not family, helpful or hurtful, wise or naive. It wasn't so much that she saw things in black-and-white as it was that for her, life had been uncomplicated to this point. He could only pray that it would remain so for her. She needed to find a guy who had a family like hers. Then they'd have a dual support system, as most Amish newlyweds did.

He didn't know why his thoughts were focused on Becca's future marriage, when to his knowledge she wasn't even stepping out, but he could see her in a house of her own. He could see her surrounded by children and wayward chickens and hound dogs. What he couldn't see was her with another man.

Which was ridiculous.

It wasn't as if she would be interested in the likes of him, even if he was in a place to look for a *fraa*.

Which he wasn't. He wasn't even close.

The last thing she needed was in-laws with a history of problems, especially ones that had become an integral part of their lives.

No. Becca Schwartz would be better off stepping out with a normal guy—one who could provide her with a normal house and farm and family.

One of the things he'd written in his book, one that he hadn't shared with her, pretty much summed up his life and how it would not be a good life for her.

Money, especially excess money, brought with it a world of trouble.

Becca tried not to laugh as Daniel climbed the steps of his front porch. Of course, he'd insisted on moving Constance and stabling her first. The mare looked quite content, if a horse could look satisfied, pleased and happy to be home.

Now he stood staring in disbelief at his house.

"How did they manage to do all of this?"

"Surely you've been to a barn raising before."

"This wasn't a barn, though."

"We do the same for houses all the time." Becca thought the place looked fantastic. There was no longer any danger of falling through the porch's floor. The railing was solid. The new paint gleamed in the bright November sunshine.

Daniel opened the screen door—then closed and opened it again. "Works better."

"Because it's a new door. I thought the

workers would be better off tearing down your old place and building a new one, but Silas King—he's usually the foreman of our work crews—said your place has good bones."

"He told me the same when he stopped by, and he described the work, but..."

"But what?"

"I didn't envision this, couldn't imagine it at all."

They walked into the house and Daniel stopped in the middle of the sitting room. He turned in a circle, looked up at the ceiling, went over and tapped the window frame, then dropped his bag on the floor and put his hands on his hips. "Where did the furniture come from?"

"That old couch?"

"Doesn't look that old."

"It was somebody's who didn't need it anymore. You know how it is with Plain people. We rarely throw things away."

He clomped into the kitchen, turned and looked at her with his mouth slightly ajar, then strode to the pantry and jerked the door open. Becca knew what he was going to see. She'd helped to stock the shelves. Rows and rows of canned goods that people had donated from their own harvest, plus paper goods and staples they'd purchased with money from the benevolence fund.

"This is terrible."

"What? That you can eat something besides oatmeal?"

Daniel sank into a chair at the table he hadn't owned before he was sick. "I knew they were going to rebuild the place, and I didn't see a way to stop them."

"Why would you?"

"But they've furnished it, given me enough food to see me through the winter..."

"You'll still need meat, fresh eggs and dairy." Becca opened the refrigerator and scanned it, then removed a small pitcher of milk. She set the kettle on the used stove that had been placed in the corner of the kitchen. "There's only enough for a couple of weeks."

Daniel's reply was a groan. When she glanced over at him, he was sitting at the table with his head in his hands.

"This tea will fix you right up. You're probably just tired."

"You don't get it. You don't understand."

She sat across from him. "Then explain it to me. Why is all of this bad?"

"Because they're giving out of what they don't have."

"Many in our community have more than enough."

"And many don't." Daniel scrubbed his hands over his face, then finally looked at her. "Many don't, and they've given part of what little they have to me. That's not right because I—"

He stopped midsentence, a pained expression on his face.

"What? You had nothing here, Daniel—except your horse and your sleeping bag and your journal. People wanted to help from day one, but you wouldn't let them. It took your coming down with the flu before you'd accept help. Now don't ruin it by letting your pride become involved."

"It's not pride."

"What is it then?"

"I can't... I can't explain why this is such a terrible thing, Becca. Just trust me. I should not have accepted this much help."

She stared at him a moment, waited until he raised those beautiful brown eyes to hers. When he did, she smiled, ducked her head and gave him a pointed look. "You can't take any of it back, so I suggest you get used to the new Daniel Glick homestead and learn to say thank you. That's all people expect."

"That's it? That's your advice? Say thank you?"

"Uh-huh. Oh, and be ready to jump in when they need help, because that's what neighbors do."

The kettle whistled, and she hopped up to fix his tea. In truth, Daniel's house only held minimal furniture now. Yes, he had a bed, a couch, an old patched recliner and a table with seating for four. He had a new roof, new siding, tight window frames and a porch where he wouldn't break his legs. He had a used propane stove and refrigerator, and when he finally made it to the mudroom, he'd see a nearly archaic wringer washing machine.

He had the minimum, but you'd think by the look on his face that people had furnished his place for an *Englisch* magazine photo op. She didn't understand that. She didn't understand his need to live so sparsely.

He seemed to be stuck on the fact that he was poor.

Her family was poor, too, but they didn't mind having food and clothing and a furnished home.

Men were a mystery to her, and Daniel Glick? Daniel was a paradox. For a guy who carried around a book and filled it with words of wisdom, she thought he had a lot of learning to do.

Chapter Eight

The next week and a half passed in a blur. Daniel went to town as soon as he felt strong enough, withdrew more money and gave it to Bishop Saul.

The good bishop simply patted him on the shoulder and assured him that he would "see it went into the benevolence fund—another anonymous donation."

On the Sunday after he moved back home, he stood up at the church meeting and thanked everyone. It was both harder and easier than he'd expected. Harder because it had been a long time since he had felt anything resembling kinship to other people. Easier because the response was laughter, cries of "We'll call you when our harvest is ready," and murmurs that at least now he could begin courting without fear of scaring off the woman.

But he had no intentions of courting.

He set himself to the work of a farmer in winter—mending fences, buying and transporting hay for Constance, and ordering seed for the spring. The first snowfall brought over a foot of white powder, and he found an old, tattered horse blanket in the loft of the barn for his mare. She tossed her head when he put it on her, but when he released her into the field it appeared she had forgiven him.

The Schwartz brood came by with sleds and insisted he accompany them to the top of a small hill at the back of the property. There was only a foot of snow on the ground, and the hill wasn't that large, but you'd have thought they were at a famous ski resort the way they carried on. He didn't think Becca could look prettier. Wrapped in what must have been her *bruder*'s coat, well-worn mittens, a bonnet and a scarf, she looked like a snow princess to him.

It was while they were having hot chocolate at his place, all seven of her younger siblings spread out on the living room couch and floor, that he realized she was up to something.

He tugged her arm and pulled her into the kitchen.

"What are you doing?"

"What do you mean what am I doing?"

"You were texting someone on Francine's phone. How does Francine even have a phone?"

"Not that it's any of your business, but it's not her phone. It's her friend's phone. You know she thinks she's on her *rumspringa*."

"She's only twelve."

"I know that. Go speak to her about it if you dare. As to who or why I was texting on it, I don't want to talk about that with you."

He scowled at her, but it did nothing to intimidate her into confessing.

Before they left, he tried talking to Clyde and David.

"Don't know," Clyde admitted. "Another one of her get-less-poor plans."

David wrapped his scarf tightly around his neck. "She's still a bit put out that Carl-the-bad-tempered-rooster hasn't brought any new baby chicks. Seems the hens are hiding from him."

"He's a nice-looking Brahma, though." Clyde ran a hand up and down his jawline, attempting to look serious and thoughtful. "Maybe we can roast him for Thanksgiving."

The two *bruders* high-fived, then turned to trudge off after their *schweschdern*. Daniel couldn't have explained what he did next—it was pure instinct. He jogged after the group and motioned Clyde toward his barn.

"Has she asked you to let her use the buggy? What I mean is, has she asked you not to take it to work?"

Clyde had been working for a big Amish farm across town—the owners were actually in another church district, but they paid well, and he was still saving for his own buggy.

"Actually, *ya*. She said she could take me to work tomorrow, use the buggy and then pick me back up in the afternoon."

"Is that unusual?"

"Can't remember her doing it before."

"So it has to do with this new plan?"

"It could. Why? Is that a problem?"

Becca had never told her family about the CBD plants. Something told him that this might be like that. Getting in over her head again. Not that Becca Schwartz needed him to follow her around and protect her. But they were friends, right? What was it she had said standing in his kitchen? *Be ready to jump in when they need help, because that's what neighbors do.*

That was exactly what he was going to do then—jump in and help.

"Go ahead and take your buggy. I'll give her a ride to town."

"You're sure?"

"Absolutely. I need to run some errands anyway."

"Sounds *gut* to me. I'll let her know."

Daniel was glad he wouldn't be there when Clyde shared the change in plans. He was pretty sure that whatever Becca was doing in town, she did not want her family to know about it.

That thought was confirmed an hour later when she came barging into the barn. "What is your problem?" Her bonnet was askew, she was only wearing one mitten, and she'd forgotten to button her coat.

Daniel had been in the middle of giving Constance her daily brush-down. He turned back toward the horse and resumed his work. "Wasn't aware I had one."

"Why did you tell Clyde you'd take me to town?"

"Because neighbors help each other. Remember?"

She tried pinning him with an aggravated look. When he didn't jump to the bait, she picked up the horse comb, walked over and commenced combing out Constance's mane.

"Why are you doing that?"

"I'm helping. That's what neighbors do."

"*Ya*, but Constance and I were doing just fine without your help." He was hoping to aggravate her, to provoke her into stepping away—or even better, leaving his barn altogether. *Their* barn. It was their barn. He had to keep reminding himself of that. Regardless, Becca looked too adorable to be standing so close to him. He moved to the other side of the mare.

"I understand." She leaned forward and smelled the mare's neck, then glanced over at him. "I was doing fine without your help. So why did you stick your nose into my affairs?"

"Because you're up to something."

"I have no idea know what you mean."

"It's another get-rich scheme. Isn't it?"

"I don't want to be rich. I just want to be less poor."

"Haven't you outgrown this absurd idea? Didn't the hemp plants teach you anything?"

"They taught me to be more careful." She raised her chin a fraction of an inch. "This is completely aboveboard."

"Oh, is it?"

"Uh-huh. I have the man's business card and everything. I even checked out his website."

"Business card? Website? Are you listening to yourself? You sound like a *youngie*."

"Look, Daniel. I know you can't understand this because you're living over here all by yourself, but I have a family—a very large family. Plus, Christmas is coming, and I want to be able to give them nice things. Is that so wrong?"

"It is if you're going to get yourself in trouble."

"I *won't* get in trouble."

They were glaring at each other over Constance's back, and the mare nodded her head as if to say, *go on...*

"Tell me what you're doing, and if it doesn't sound dangerous, I'll let you borrow Constance and my buggy and go by yourself."

"I do not need your permission to go to town alone."

"Of course not."

"But it would be convenient to use your horse and buggy."

"Exactly."

"Fine." She put the comb back on the shelf, then walked over to stand next to him. Pulling a piece of paper from her pocket, she unfolded it and pushed it into his hands.

"What is this?" Daniel's thoughts scrambled as he stared down at the sheet of paper. It showed a picture of an Amish woman with two small children walking away from the camera. There was the slightest indication that the woman was about to look back over her shoulder and smile at the person taking the photograph.

As he read the words below the picture, he thought his head might pop right off his shoulders.

Plain & Simple Glamour Shots
Tastefully Done
Earn extra money for your farm,
family or community

"Tell me you are not going to do this."

"Why wouldn't I?"

"Because we don't pose for pictures."

"Look. It says right here, Tastefully Done. When I checked the web page, there were quite a few testimonials from women saying they'd worked for two to three hours and earned plenty of extra money."

"Becca, look at me."

She reluctantly raised her eyes to his.

"Don't do this. You can't believe this piece of paper or that website. Anyone could make up those things."

"But why would they? See, I've thought of that, but why would they make it up? There's no reason to. They simply want photographs for their magazines, and since it never shows our face, and we're even allowed to wear Plain clothing... Well, what's the harm?"

Daniel handed the sheet of paper back to her, but instead of resuming the work with Constance, he walked out of the stall into the main room of the barn. He was very aware that if he said the wrong thing, Becca would go off and do what she wanted to do. She wanted to believe this was legitimate. Maybe it was. Who could say?

But a warning alarm in his heart told him it could be dangerous.

Finally, he turned toward her. "Let me go with you."

"What?"

"Let me go with you. When are you supposed to meet him?"

"Tomorrow, but I don't need you with me."

"What time?"

"None of your business."

"Let me go with you, and if everything seems legit, then I'll go wait for you in the buggy."

"In the cold? You're going to wait in the buggy in the cold for hours?"

"Sure."

"Ridiculous. You'd probably end up sick again. Plus, there's no reason for you to do such a thing. You could simply wait on the other side of the coffee shop."

"That's where you're meeting? Which coffee shop?"

"The Kitchen Cupboard, in Davis Mercantile, but I don't need someone watching over me, Daniel. I'm a grown woman."

"Oh, *ya*." He rubbed his chin, then shot a hopefully serious look her way. "But I need some supplies in town, and I do love a *gut* cup of coffee."

He thought she'd be offended.

He expected her to storm away after forbidding him to come.

Instead, she walked over to where he was, standing close enough that he took a step back and bumped into the wall.

"You're worried about me."

"Well, you know. Neighbors..."

"Helping neighbors. I heard you before, but this is different. Are you getting sweet on me, Daniel?"

He crossed his arms and scowled at her. "Stop it."

"What? A girl has a right to be flattered."

So that was her plan. She'd embarrass him, and then he'd call it off. Only he wasn't falling for that. He was going to stay focused on the objective, which was to see Becca safely through another crazy scheme.

"What if I am, Becca? Are you interested?" Now he stepped toward her, only she didn't back away as he'd expected. Instead, she looked up at him, laughter in her eyes.

"We'll continue this conversation tomorrow after my meeting."

"Sure. Okay."

"After you see that I am a capable, independent woman who doesn't need to be looked after."

There was that spunk he was expecting to hear from her.

"But I have to say, I'm flattered that you care so much."

More bait. He wasn't going to respond. She was almost to the door, when he thought to call out to her. "What time should I pick you up?"

"Nine o'clock sharp."

With a backward wave of her hand, she was gone, leaving Daniel to wonder what he'd just gotten himself into.

The next morning, Becca stood staring at her four dresses. She wanted to wear her best dress to town, but she knew that would make her *mamm* suspicious. She only wore that dress on church Sundays. Best to wear her second-best and avoid the scrutiny. She did take a little extra time with her hair and *kapp*, not that the man would be photographing her today, and besides, it would only be from the back when he did start taking pictures.

Still, she'd like to look her best. So she made sure that her hair was braided nicely and tucked into her *kapp* except for a soft fringe around her face. She didn't have any makeup, had never had much of a *rumspringa* herself. She momentarily thought about checking with Francine to see if she had any blush or powder or lip gloss, but that would only be encouraging her *schweschder*'s rebellious ways.

"It is what it is," she murmured to the small mirror, then hurried downstairs.

Her *mamm* was too busy with Thanksgiving preparations to notice that Becca was up to something.

"You're sure you don't mind getting all these supplies for me while you're in town?"

Becca stared down at the long list in surprise. Her *mamm* wanted all these things? Were they feeding their family or the entire neighborhood? And where had the money come from? As if reading her mind, her *mamm* pressed a wad of bills into her hand. "Clyde's been helping out and your *dat* was paid for his work over at the factory. *Gotte* provides, Becca."

"Yes, he does," she said, but what she was thinking was that *Gotte* provided for those who worked. Didn't it say that somewhere in the Bible? She'd have to ask the bishop next time she saw him. Regardless, she planned to contribute some to the holiday meal herself, or if she didn't have any money that soon, she could at least help purchase Christmas gifts for her siblings.

Her thoughts were focused on that as she helped with breakfast, scooting everyone off to school and cleaning up the kitchen. She was surprised when she heard the clatter of buggy wheels and realized Daniel was there.

"I'm so happy that you two are doing things together, dear." Her *mamm* didn't even try to hide her enormous smile.

"It's not like that."

"Often it's not...until it is."

Becca thought of arguing, but she had a feeling that the more she protested, the more she sounded like a teenage girl with a crush on the new boy in town. So instead, she kissed her *mamm* on the cheek, snagged her coat and hurried outside.

Daniel was speaking to her *dat*, who was grinning as if Christmas had already come. She arrived in time to hear him ask, "What did the farmer say when he lost one of his cows?"

"Hmm. I can't imagine." Daniel looked at her and wriggled his eyebrows.

"He said, *What a miss-steak!*"

Her *dat* would have launched right into another joke, if Becca hadn't intervened.

"I guess we better hurry so we make it to town before the stores get too busy."

Daniel looked skyward, as if he expected help from that direction. At least he didn't argue with her in front of her *dat*.

"So they don't know?" he asked in a low voice.

"Of course they don't know."

"Don't you feel guilty about that?"

"Did you tell your parents everything when you were twenty-four?"

Daniel scrubbed his hand across his face. "*Nein*. I didn't, but this isn't about me."

It was a beautiful day, but Becca could hardly appreciate it with butterflies fluttering around in her stomach. She told herself that it was about the interview, but it was also about the man sitting next to her. When had she begun to think of Daniel in *that* way? She shook off the thoughts and suggested he drop her off at the mercantile's front door.

"I thought we'd walk in together."

"And I thought it would be better if it didn't look like we were a couple."

"Fine."

"Fine."

The scowl on his face was almost comical, but he didn't argue with her. She didn't bother looking back as she slammed the buggy door shut. She could do this. She could be an independent woman, and she could show Daniel Glick that she knew how to take advantage of a good business opportunity when she saw one.

She hurried into the mercantile, past JoJo's Pretzels and into the coffee shop. The place smelled like baked goods and freshly ground coffee, and the shelves were covered with packaged teas, coffee and mugs. A mere eight tables were scattered throughout the space, so it was pretty easy to spot the man who had given her the flyer when she was last in town.

"Hi, I'm Becca."

"And I'm Sean Wilson. Would you like a coffee?"

"Ya. Danki." She told him how she liked her coffee and tried not to crinkle her nose at the smell of his too-strong cologne. Sean Wilson used a little too much hair gel, too. In fact, without his baseball cap on, he seemed older than she'd first thought. Why would anyone comb their hair over and plaster it down? The look was somewhat ridiculous, but then she supposed *Englisch* had different styles than Amish. She knew the women did, so perhaps the men did, as well.

She settled into the table he'd been waiting for her at, while he went to purchase her drink. There was a stack of flyers on the table, or perhaps they were simply full-size photographs. The first was the one she had seen, where the Amish woman and two children were walking away.

Becca glanced up, confirmed that Sean Wilson's attention was with the barista, and scanned through the pictures. Only the top three were similar in nature. As she quickly glanced through the others, she was alarmed to see that they were women looking directly at the camera, some in Amish clothes, some not in Amish clothes, and some in poses that struck her as quite flirtatious.

Her mouth went suddenly dry, and she could feel her heartbeat pulsing in her temples.

It was really none of her business what types of photographs Sean's company used in their advertisements. Didn't she see the same thing on every *Englisch* magazine at the store? She would never pose in such a way, and she would make that quite clear.

As Sean walked back toward the table with her coffee, he passed Daniel. Daniel turned, gave her a thumbs-up, then ordered his own coffee. By the time Becca was able to direct the conversation to any possible work, Daniel was seated two tables behind them facing her. Close enough in case she needed him, but far enough away to give them some semblance of privacy.

"I'm glad you responded to our ad." Sean restacked the photographs. If he noticed she'd looked through them, he didn't remark on it. "How long have you wanted to be a model?"

Becca nearly spilled her coffee. "Oh, I have no desire to be a model."

"No?"

"*Nein*. I mean, no. I'm willing to have a tasteful photograph taken, like this one on top." She tapped the stack of photographs. Best to get this out in the open now. "But I'd never pose like some of those beneath—where the woman is looking right at the camera or where she has her shirt off her shoulder."

"You're shy."

"I'm not shy in the least, but I wouldn't go against our *Ordnung*."

"I see." He sipped his coffee and studied her. "You have beautiful features."

Becca didn't know how to answer that,

so she didn't. Then she remembered something her *dat* had said recently. *Straight ahead is shorter than round about.* Best to plunge in and get this over with.

"Mr. Wilson—"

"Sean."

She nodded, but she didn't use his first name. It seemed too personal—as if they were friends, and she wasn't at all sure about that.

"The question isn't about my features, not really, since any pictures I would do for you would be facing away from the camera. The question is simply where, when and how much you're paying."

"I like a gal who gets straight to the point."

Gal? Did he just call her a gal? Something about this meeting wasn't going as planned. The butterflies in her stomach had switched to the feeling of a lump—something in between having eaten too much and having a stomach bug.

"I rather like straight answers."

"All right." He again straightened the stack of photographs, then met her gaze head-on. "The truth is that I have plenty of women who are willing to put on a bonnet—"

"It's a *kapp.*"

"Plenty of gals who will wear a badly designed dress and walk away from the camera. I can get that any day of the week. Would we pay you for it? Probably not, but you'd at least be gaining some experience and photo shoots that you could add to your portfolio."

"I don't need experience, and I don't have a portfolio."

Sean continued, as if she hadn't interrupted him. "What pays better—you'd be surprised how much—is for you to let us give you some fashionable clothes, let your hair down, literally, and then allow some private viewings of your photography shoot."

Becca stood up so quickly that she jostled the coffee out of both of their cups, right onto the stack of photographs. She didn't care. In fact, she had the irrational thought that she'd like to pick up his stupid stack of pictures and toss them on the floor.

Some part of her mind recognized that Daniel had stood and was moving toward them. She didn't pause. She wasn't waiting for her knight in shining armor to arrive and save her from the bad man. She was ready to give the bad man a piece of her mind.

"This is not what you advertised, and it is not what I agreed to."

Oh, if only she could wipe the smirk off his face.

"You should be ashamed of yourself, Mr. Wilson. If that's even your real name. You can be sure that my bishop will be hearing about this—"

"And the police." Daniel's steady presence beside her calmed her quaking nerves.

"Yes, and the police."

Sean Wilson laughed. "Don't you think you're overreacting?"

"*Nein*. I don't. What I do think is that some of the girls in these pictures were underage, and I'm wondering if you had their parents' permission to photograph them."

A cold and hostile expression passed over Sean's face. "Don't even think about messing with me, lady. Just because you think you're too good…"

"She is too good." Daniel was now standing shoulder to shoulder with Becca. "And we both think it would be best if you leave now. Or would you like me to call the owner over? We'd be happy to tell her that you're running a business—very likely an illegal business—in her coffee shop."

Sean Wilson was already gathering up his things. Without another word, he stormed out the door. Becca walked to the window while Daniel went to speak with the shop owner. When he returned, he asked, "Are you okay?"

"Ya."

"What's that?" He nodded toward the folded sheet of paper in her hands. It was the flyer that Sean had given her when she'd first met him, and on the back, she'd written the type of car he was driving, as well as his license plate number.

"I think we need to go to the police again."

Chapter Nine

Daniel directed Constance toward the police station. Once there, they told the receptionist that they'd like to speak to an officer, and then sat down in the waiting area. Just like before.

Becca had been completely silent on the way over. Now she looked at him, misery etched on her face, and admitted, "I feel like a fool."

"Don't do that."

"Don't do what?"

"Don't take someone else's poor actions and blame yourself for them."

The worry lines between her eyes eased.

She didn't quite smile, but neither was she staring blankly at her hands. It was an improvement.

"Is that something written in your book?"

"Nein."

"Maybe it should be."

Before she could tease him more about his notebook, Officer Raquel Sanchez appeared in the doorway. "You two again."

Becca and Daniel stood.

"More CBD plants?"

"Nein." Becca stepped forward, and Daniel was relieved to see that some of the color had returned to her face. "But I think we need to report a crime."

Sanchez tilted her head, then said, "Better come on back."

Daniel noticed the other desks in the large room were still a mess, and Sanchez's was still a beacon of cleanliness and order.

There was one chair sitting next to Sanchez's desk, and she moved over another. She pulled out a pad of paper and a pen, then said, "Okay. Tell it to me from the beginning."

Becca did, and Daniel didn't interrupt. Sanchez wrote down a few notes, then asked, "Did you feel threatened in any way?"

"He seemed threatening to me." Daniel glanced at Becca who nodded once. "Especially after Becca told him he had misrepresented himself on the advertising sheet."

"And are you sure the photographs were of underage girls?"

"They seemed awfully young to me, but here's the thing…" Becca glanced nervously to her right and left, then lowered her voice, though they were the only ones in the room. "I think I recognized a couple of the girls. I think they're Amish girls, from our community. At least I'm pretty sure one is, and I know she's only twelve—same age as my *schweschder*."

"Okay." Officer Sanchez sat back in her chair, causing it to creak. "It's not illegal for teenage girls to have modeling gigs. On the other hand, it is illegal to misrepresent yourself, to coerce girls into modeling that they're not comfortable with, and you definitely need parental permission if the girl is a minor." She sat forward, elbows on her desk, fingers steepled. "Are you willing to give me the name of the girl you saw?"

"I wouldn't want to get her in trouble with her parents."

"I understand." Sanchez waited a moment, then picked up a pen and tapped the sheet where she'd written the information regarding Wilson's car. "On the other hand, you might be protecting her."

"Protecting her in what way?"

"Are you familiar with human trafficking?"

"I've read a few articles about it."

Daniel shifted in his seat. "Our community in Pennsylvania was briefed on it by local law enforcement. They were afraid Plain girls might be an easy target."

Sanchez sat back, causing her chair to squeak. "We've had chatter lately about a human trafficking ring that has set up along the I-90 corridor. Those girls sometimes get lured in thinking that they've signed up for a modeling job, only to find that much more is expected of them."

"That's terrible."

"If we could talk to this girl, see what she has to say...then possibly we'd have enough to put an All Points Bulletin out for Sean Wilson."

Becca glanced at Daniel.

"Think if it was Francine," he said, which he knew would push her toward doing the right thing.

Becca gave Sanchez the girl's name and directions to her house.

"Can you give me some idea how her parents will react to this?"

"Her *dat*'s pretty strict, and her *mamm* is... I guess you could say she's a bit timid."

"Okay. This is in your church district?"

"*Ya.*"

"And Saul Lapp is your bishop?"

"He is."

"Then I'll swing by and speak with Bishop Saul first, see if he'd like to go with me. In these instances, it can help to keep everyone calm and reasonable if we have a clergyman along."

"Is there anything else we can do?" Becca stood, pulled her purse strap tight over her shoulder and stepped closer to Daniel. He liked that—that she would find some comfort from his presence.

"Nothing I can think of at the moment, but I appreciate your coming in. A lot of people wouldn't. They'd just think they misread the situation or that they were overeager to make a buck. The fact that you were willing to come forward and talk to us—it shows a real level of maturity. It shows how much you care for your community." Sanchez walked them out of the office and thanked them again. She promised to let them know if there were any developments in the case.

When they stepped outside, Becca stood there on the steps, her face turned up to the November sunshine.

"Are you okay?"

She closed her eyes and breathed in deeply before answering. "Feels like this day has already lasted forever."

"Nope. Only—" he checked his watch "—ninety minutes."

"Unbelievable."

"We still have time to go shopping for the things on your *mamm*'s list. Only two days until Thanksgiving. I imagine she's going to be pretty busy cooking the next few days."

"Thanksgiving." Becca hooked her arm through his and they walked toward the buggy together. "I have a lot to be thankful for this year."

"Even though the job didn't work out?"

"Even though." She turned to him as he opened the buggy's door. "*Danki*, Daniel. It was *gut* having you there with me. I like to think of myself as an independent woman—"

"You *are* an independent woman."

"But even so, having a friend along is a *gut* thing. *Danki* for being there for me today."

He felt his face flush, thought of kissing her, then wondered if he'd gone a little crazy to consider doing such a thing in public in broad daylight. "Just being a *gut* neighbor."

She hopped up into the buggy. He untethered Constance, then climbed into the driver's seat. They were nearly to the store when Becca said, "I owe you."

"You do not."

"And I mean to pay you back. You've helped me out of a tight spot twice now."

"Nothing to pay back." He could tell that her mood had shifted, though, and that the spunky, playful Becca was nearly back. "But if you did, um, pay me back... what did you have in mind?"

She rubbed her hands up and down her

cheeks, patting them slightly. "Oh, I don't know. Maybe some turkey, dressing, cranberry sauce…"

"Homemade?"

"Of course it's homemade. Then there will be the vegetable casseroles, fresh bread, cakes and pies."

"Stop," he groaned. "I haven't had your *mamm*'s cooking for almost two weeks."

"Still having canned soup at your place?"

"Guilty as charged."

"So you wouldn't be averse to accepting a dinner invitation?"

"I wouldn't."

Becca laughed. "We were going to ask you anyway. *Mamm* reminded me before you showed up this morning."

"Is that so?"

"*Ya.* You're like an honorary family member, Daniel."

For reasons he didn't want to examine, a lump formed in his throat. He swallowed past it and tried to focus on the road. Becca was headstrong and somewhat naive in certain situations, especially those outside a Plain community. She was also kind, free-spirited, and passionate about life.

He couldn't think of anywhere he'd rather be on Thanksgiving, anywhere better than with the young woman sitting beside him and her family.

Becca pulled out the shopping list her *mamm* had given her. They might live on one of the worst farms in Shipshe, but on Thursday they would thank the Lord for the things they had. They'd pray and eat and laugh and be together. And that wasn't a bad way to spend Thanksgiving. In fact, looking at Daniel, who was suddenly grinning like a child on his birthday, she realized that she was actually looking forward to the holiday.

The next hour passed pleasantly enough as she and Daniel filled the cart with items for the Thanksgiving meal.

"I'd like to help pay for this."

"Oh, no, you won't."

"But…"

"Uh-uh. Not going to happen. We don't ask guests to dinner and then have them pay their way." She pulled out the bills her *mamm* had given her and paid the cashier.

Fortunately, the buggy Daniel had purchased had a storage compartment mounted on the back. Between that space and the back seat, they were able to store all of the supplies. Once they were back in the buggy, Becca realized she would need to tell her parents about today. She didn't have to, but she'd feel better if she did. Keeping things from them only made her feel childish and on edge. Better to have the hard conversation.

She chuckled lightly.

"What's funny over there?"

"I was thinking of something you could put in your book of wisdom."

"Oh yeah?"

"Have the hard conversation."

"I don't get it."

She turned in the buggy, her back against the space where the seat met the door so that she could better watch him. Daniel was a handsome man, and he was older than she was. It seemed that in some areas he was pretty inexperienced—especially when it came to relationships.

"Explain it to me," he prodded. "If I'm going to put it in my notebook, I need to understand it."

"Okay. Say that you hire my *bruder* to come over and help you plant your field."

"I did hire your *bruders* to help me plant my field."

"Uh-huh, but say they did a terrible job."

"They did a great job."

"Work with me here."

"All right. I'm pretending they did a terrible job."

"Now, would you tell them so? Or would you thank them, pay them and send them on their way."

"Hmm. I'd be tempted to do the latter, and then just not ask them to help again."

"Exactly!" Becca reached over and patted his arm. "I knew you would get it."

"But I don't get it."

"Look. If you did what you just said—thanked them, paid them, sent them on their way, then how would they learn? They'd go on being terrible farm workers, and word would get around, and then they wouldn't be able to find a job."

"But if I had the hard conversation…"

"Which is difficult to do because you don't want to hurt anyone's feelings, and it's awkward, and you could be wrong."

"I'm pretty sure I know a bad farm worker when I see one."

"Right, and doesn't the Bible say to speak the truth in love?"

"I believe it does."

"Only you have to search your heart first—to see if it is love that's motivating you or if it's something else."

Daniel directed Constance down their road, and then into Becca's lane.

"I could have walked from your place."

"With all these groceries?"

"Oh, right."

He pulled Constance to a stop, set the brake, then turned to study Becca.

"So this hard conversation that you're about to have... I assume it's about what happened at the coffee shop."

"It is." Becca watched Daniel closely. She didn't see any condemnation there. He hadn't said a word about how silly she'd been. No I-told-you-so. Just compassion.

"Would you like me to stay, provide emotional backup?"

She leaned forward, kissed him on the cheek, then patted his arm again when he blushed bright red. "*Danki*, but this is something I need to do on my own."

The next two days passed in a flurry of preparation. In addition to Daniel, they'd have *Onkel* Jeremiah, plus Abigail and her family. Becca kept rechecking her tally, and each time she ended up with sixteen. Or was it seventeen?

"Stop with the list." Her *mamm* reached across and tugged on the sheet of paper, then set it out of her reach. "We've prepared plenty of food, and we'll make room for whoever shows up. It's going to be fine, Becca."

"I guess." Her mind was spinning with all the things to do before the luncheon, which was traditionally held around one thirty.

"What do you think it means to be Plain?"

That pulled Becca out of her planning mode as if she'd been splashed with cold water.

"Huh?"

Her *mamm* stood, refilled their coffee cups, then sat back down. Her *dat* and Clyde and David were in the barn caring for the animals, and the rest of the family was still asleep. It was the precious part of the day before the pandemonium started. In a family as big as theirs, every day held its share of chaos, but Thanksgiving more than others.

"Tell me what you think it means to be Plain."

"I've already joined the church, *Mamm*. I know what Plain means."

"Right. I know you've been through the bishop's classes, and I'm pleased that you did commit yourself to the Lord, our church and our way of life."

"But?"

"But what do you think it means to be Plain?" Her *mamm* smiled over the rim of her coffee mug. "Humor me."

"Okay. Well, it means our life is simpler, that we strive to be *in* the world but not *of* it, and that we choose to do things the old way. We do sometimes embrace change, like the solar panels that are going up on everyone's houses, but we do so carefully and slowly."

"*Gut* answer."

"*Danki.*" Why did she feel like she'd received an A on a school paper? She sipped her coffee and tried to guess what her *mamm* was up to, because she was definitely up to something. Her expression was smiling, but her eyes were quite serious.

"We strive for simplicity." Her *mamm*'s voice was soft, almost as if she were speaking to herself. "But with our large families, sometimes life is anything but simple."

"You can say that again."

Her *mamm* leaned forward, as if she was about to share a secret. "The simple part is in your attitude, Becca. Our lives are as complicated as anyone's, but if we keep our focus on what matters and don't allow ourselves to be caught up in the whirlwind of modern living, then we can have the peace that many strive for."

"You're telling me to forget about the seating chart."

"It'll never work, and it doesn't matter."

"I suppose." For some reason, she was especially concerned about the holiday meal going well this year. "I guess I want today to be perfect."

"Things will never be perfect. Perfect is overrated."

"I'll take your word for it."

Her *mamm* stood, walked to the sink and then came back and stood behind Becca's chair. She put her hands gently on Becca's shoulders, leaned forward and kissed the top of her head. It felt like a blessing of sorts, and for reasons Becca couldn't have explained, it brought tears to her eyes. "Enjoy today. We're only able to experience each day once, and it'll pass in the blink of an eye."

Then her *dat* came in, and her siblings stumbled to the table, and they were soon praying over the light breakfast and the day to come.

But suddenly Becca's mind stopped racing.

She forgot to worry about the next minute.

She allowed herself to enjoy the present one.

Enjoy today. It'll pass in the blink of an eye.

Definitely something that Daniel needed to write in his journal.

Maybe it was because Daniel had lived in their house for ten days when he was sick.

Or maybe it was because he'd grown accustomed to having all of Becca's *schweschdern* and *bruders* around. It could have even been that he missed her *dat*'s jokes.

Whatever the reason, Daniel relaxed the minute that he arrived at the Schwartz home. Becca wouldn't let him pay for the groceries, but she couldn't stop him from bringing food to the meal. Everyone did that. Daniel had gone back to town on Wednesday and purchased everything he could think of that might go with the meal Becca and her *mamm* were cooking.

Now, as David and Eli helped him carry

the sacks into the house, both Becca and her *mamm* stopped to stare at him.

"What is all of that?"

"Oh, just some...you know. Food. And stuff."

Becca gave him a glare that seemed to say, "Didn't we talk about this?"

But her *mamm* only walked over, kissed him on the cheek and said, *"Danki*, Daniel. That was very thoughtful."

Hannah and Isabelle had started to paw through the groceries, and both squealed when they found the gallons of ice cream.

"Six? You bought six gallons of ice cream?" Becca walked over to him, stood close enough that Daniel could smell the scent of the shampoo she'd used, and peered up into his face. "Did you get a little carried away?"

"Well, there was a special, and I didn't know what flavor everyone liked."

"Lucky for us, looks like you bought every flavor they had."

"Is there room in the..."

"Freezer? *Ya.* The girls will show you where it is."

The freezer was gas-powered and old, but it kept the food cold. Hannah and Isabelle led him out to the mudroom, he stuck the ice cream way down in the bottom, and they returned to the kitchen in time to find that Georgia and Francine had found the games he'd purchased.

"A new board game, and look—it's a Plain version." Georgia pushed up her glasses as she stared at the box. "I can be the horse."

"Then I get to be the lamb." Francine was actually laughing, something she hadn't done much of lately. For the day, at least, perhaps she could forget her focus on her *rumspringa.*

There were also three types of card games—Uno, Skipbo and Dutch Blitz.

"There must have been a sale in the game aisle, too." Becca tossed him a knowing look.

But Daniel understood that she didn't

really know his secret. She thought he'd simply been caught up in the holiday spirit and thrown caution to the wind. The truth was that he'd been looking for a way to pay the Schwartz family back for taking care of him, and today seemed like a natural way to do that.

Eli lined the liters of soda on the counter. "We never have soda, and hardly ever have ice cream."

"*Ya*, but you have your *mamm*'s cooking."

"True." Eli tapped one of the bottles. "Maybe tonight we can make root beer floats, after I beat you at chess."

"Dream on, kid."

Daniel thought it was funny that the boy liked chess nearly as much as he liked baseball. Perhaps it was just the playing that he liked, anticipating the next move, trying to outthink someone. He was athletic, but he also had a good mind. There was no telling what the lad would grow up to be.

Eli was already heading toward the chessboard, but Samuel walked into the room and claimed he needed help outside. As Daniel followed him, Becca's dad admitted, "Need to use up some of their energy. Plus, it helps Sarah to have them out from underfoot for an hour or so."

Daniel didn't know if his *dat* had ever done that for his *mamm*. He didn't think so. At least he didn't remember it. His parents' marriage had been strained for so many years—by the inheritance and the choices their children were making, maybe even by the way the community treated them differently—that he really couldn't remember a holiday like the one Becca's family was enjoying.

In Becca's family, everyone seemed to actually like each other.

If he ever married, he'd give up every dollar in his bank account to have this sort of home and this sort of relationship. He hadn't thought it was possible. He hadn't believed that people genuinely cared for each other so much. But as they walked to the south pasture and everyone scattered looking for items to place in the Thanksgiving bowl, he started to believe that he'd been wrong.

An hour later they were back in the house. *Onkel* Jeremiah had arrived while they were gone, and he'd stoked up the fire in the big stove that heated the sitting room. The place felt warm and cozy, and if his stomach wasn't growling Daniel might have been tempted to sit on the couch and nap a bit. But then Abigail and Aaron arrived with their two sons. Abigail was now eight months pregnant, and though she was obviously uncomfortable, it seemed that there was an aura of happiness around her.

And why wouldn't there be?

Aaron obviously doted on her, and they were expecting their third child. He wasn't too surprised to see her slip a small knitted bootie into the Thanksgiving bowl.

Becca and her *mamm* hurried from the

kitchen and took their place in the hap-
hazard circle. Becca had explained this
tradition to him, but seeing it firsthand
was an entirely different experience. The
sitting room wasn't especially large, but
they were all seated together. Everyone
was hungry because of their light breakfast, but no one complained. The feast to
come would more than make up for any
current hunger pains.

Onkel Jeremiah sat in a rocker, with his
Bible open in his lap. "The Lord be with
you," he said.

"And also with you." Hannah and Isabelle practically bounced as they recited
the age-old words with the rest of their
family.

"This year I thought we'd read Psalm 107."

The murmurs around Daniel varied from
"That's a *gut* one" to "Have we read that
before?" to "I hope it's short." That last
was from Clyde, and instead of being in
trouble, he elicited laughs from everyone.

Then Jeremiah began to read, his voice

rich and deep and filled with more wisdom than Daniel could write into his book if he lived another fifty years.

"O give thanks unto the Lord, for He is good; for His mercy endureth forever."

They all quieted, settled, focused.

"Let the redeemed of the Lord say so, whom He hath redeemed from the hand of the enemy..."

Daniel felt suddenly redeemed. He was nearly overpowered by a feeling of humility.

"And gathered them out of the lands, from the east, and from the west, from the north, and from the south. They wandered in the wilderness in a solitary way..."

Daniel had done exactly that. His wilderness had been of his own making, though. His solitary way had been a choice. He understood that now, and the understanding lifted a weight off his shoulders that he hadn't realized he'd been carrying.

He must have spaced out, because Jeremiah closed his Bible and quoted the last verse—a verse that seemed written especially for Daniel. "Whoso is wise, and will observe these things, even they shall understand the loving kindness of the Lord."

Amens circled the room, and Samuel offered a short prayer, and then it was time for the Thanksgiving bowl.

Becca loved the old ceramic bowl that sat in the middle of the table. Her *mamm* had explained that it belonged to Becca's great-grandmother, and that it was used before there was running water—when they would place a pitcher of water and a bowl on the nightstand so that in the morning you could splash cold, clean water on your face.

They didn't have many things in their home. The furniture was tattered after years of use. There were no fancy lanterns or store-bought lap blankets or machine-woven rugs. Most of what they had was homemade or used. Somehow none of that mattered when she looked at the Thanksgiving bowl brimming with items.

"Everyone has placed an item in the bowl, *ya*?"

Each person in the room nodded. Samuel passed the bowl to his wife, who put her hand in, pulled an item out without looking, and smiled. "This seems to be a baby bootie, and I believe that it's from Abigail, who is grateful for the child soon to be born."

"That was too easy," Eli insisted, but he took the bowl from his *mamm*, shut his eyes and pulled out a book. "Ha. This must be from Georgia, and I think I remember her saying that her teacher gave it to her for helping all semester at school."

And so the bowl was passed around the room, each person pulling out an item and guessing who was grateful for the thing and what it represented.

Daniel pulled out a wooden car that one of Abigail's boys had put into the bowl.

Georgia pulled out the newspaper clipping of a buggy. Everyone knew that was Clyde's item.

"Once he owns his own horse and buggy, he'll be able to go out every night with Melinda," David teased.

When it was Becca's turn, she pulled out a bright red rooster feather. "This could only belong to Carl-the-bad-tempered-rooster, and I can't imagine who would..."

But then she noticed Daniel staring at the floor, trying not to laugh.

"Daniel? And why would you be thankful for my unruly rooster?"

"Don't you remember the day I met you? You were trying to fend him off with a rake." Which started everyone laughing and telling stories of Carl. It wasn't until they'd dispersed to the kitchen that Becca realized Daniel hadn't explained exactly what he was grateful for. "A rooster?"

"Not exactly." He pulled her back into the living room, making sure they were alone, and then kissed her softly on the lips. "I'm thankful for you, Becca. Every single day."

Chapter Ten

The time between Thanksgiving and Christmas passed like a blur in front of Becca's eyes. Every trite expression she'd read about being in love felt like a reality.

Her feet barely touched the ground.

Her stomach was filled with butterflies.

She'd find herself putting the milk in the cabinet and the fresh baked bread in the refrigerator.

If her family noticed, they didn't tease her about it, but everyone was busy with Christmas preparations, as well as the up-coming school program. She was grateful that no one's attention was on her.

No one's except Daniel's.

They enjoyed walks through his fields.

He told her his plans for spring crops.

They took buggy rides for no other reason than that the days were fine, the winter sunshine was beautiful and they wanted to be together.

Twice more he kissed her—once in the barn and another time in the buggy.

She found herself wishing she kept a journal, so she could write down each precious memory. But she knew she'd never forget.

Was she falling in love with Daniel Glick?

Was he falling in love with her?

Beneath those questions lay a more difficult one. If they were, and if he asked her to marry, was she willing to accept a life of poverty? It was the only thing to mar her happiness—knowing that if she agreed to a life with Daniel, she'd be turning her back on any chance to help her family financially.

Not that he would dissuade her from her get-less-poor schemes, but Becca was old enough to understand how these things went. They'd marry, and before five years were passed, they'd have three children. She'd continue having children for the next ten to fifteen years, as many as the Lord saw fit to give them.

And part of her wanted that. Each time she looked at her *schweschder* Abigail, she thought, *That could be me this time next year.* Her heart would flutter and she'd have to step outside to gather her thoughts.

But what of their living conditions?

Was she ready to give up on the dream that they might one day have more?

Someone else might chastise her for focusing on material things—someone who hadn't lived her life, someone who had those material things she wasn't supposed to hope for.

But she'd been poor a long time.

She understood what it was like to sit

with a feverish sibling, hoping her temperature would drop so they wouldn't need the doctor—wouldn't have to dip into the benevolence fund yet again.

She'd eaten soup not just for days on end, but once for an entire month as they waited for the harvest from their own garden, and money from the crops, and the chance to hunt for deer so they'd have meat.

In some ways, she thought Daniel's situation might be worse than theirs. He was undoubtedly as poor as they were, but at times he'd spend money as if he had baskets full of it. The items weren't for himself, but did it make any difference? It seemed to Becca that he was purchasing things for others while he still had no money to buy furniture for his own house. He'd recently added two lawn chairs to his living room furniture. That was it. No coffee table. No bookcase. No rocking chair.

Was she ready to go into even deeper poverty?

Then he'd show up on her front porch with a basket of pine cones or a jar of red berries, or simply wanting to read to her from his journal, and she'd think, "Yes. I could live that way. If two people really care for one another, they can endure any hardship."

It was her first thought each morning and her last thought as she drifted off to sleep. Then nineteen days after Thanksgiving and one week before Christmas, she fell asleep in her room at the back of the house and dreamed of walking through a mist.

She seemed to hear her family as if from a great distance, along with urgent barking from Cola the beagle. There was something she needed to find in the fog. There was someone she needed to see and talk to. She walked on and on, with occasional dark shadows looming close to her. Once she caught a glimpse of Carl-the-bad-tempered-rooster. A bird had set to beeping somewhere close to her. At other times, sounds that she couldn't distinguish reached her.

Her pulse began to accelerate and her skin went clammy.

She began to run, with no real destination in mind—only the certain knowledge that she needed to get away and she needed to call for help.

But her voice made no sound.

She couldn't outrun the ever-thickening fog.

She was still alone and afraid and unsure what to do next.

A loud bang caused her to sit up in bed. The fog that had plagued her throughout the dream surrounded her, and she could hear Cola's desperate barking in the distance. She pulled in a deep breath, which only caused her to cough and gasp for air as she dropped to the floor.

It wasn't fog.

And it wasn't a dream.

It was a fire.

The beeping came from the fire alarms

they'd placed in key places throughout the house.

She shared a room with Francine and Georgia. They must still be here. They wouldn't have left without her. She put out a hand, bumped into the door of their room and held her palm against it. It wasn't hot. Good.

Everything she'd been taught in school about fires came back to her in a rush.

Check the door—not the doorknob— with your fingertips.

Smoke is toxic, so stay low.

If you can't safely leave a room, keep smoke out by covering cracks.

Signal for help with a flashlight.

But they were at the back of the house. Who would see them? Did anyone else even know that there was a fire? Surely someone could hear the dog barking.

She tried yelling, but it only made her cough louder and longer and deeper. The sound woke Francine and Georgia, who also began coughing.

Becca grabbed three garments from the cubbies that held their clothes. She made her way to their beds, pulled them onto the floor and spoke in their ears.

"Stay low. Hold this to your mouth. Francine, keep your other hand on my back. Georgia, you do the same to Francine. We're going to the window."

Twice they ran into beds and realized they were going the wrong way, but finally, they made it to the window. She fumbled with the latch, and then as she pushed the window open, air rushed into the room—good air, though still tinged with the smell of fire.

Becca gulped it as if it were water, filled her lungs and then turned to help her *schweschdern* climb outside.

"Go to the front of the house. Wait by the old tree. Stay there until someone comes."

"But where are you...?"

"Just go." But instead of pushing, she pulled both girls to her, kissed them each on the cheeks, and then helped them climb through the open window.

She couldn't go. Not yet. Because she was thinking of Clyde, whose room was around the corner from hers, a room that had no window.

Daniel was in a sound sleep when he woke to the smell of smoke.

His first thought was the barn. He pulled on his shoes, pants and a shirt, grabbed the blanket off his bed in case he needed to beat out flames, and hurried outside, praying that Constance wasn't trapped.

His barn was fine, silhouetted against the December sky by the half moon—a moon that provided enough light for him to see smoke coming from the Schwartz place.

He didn't bother going back inside for his coat. Instead, he dashed through their shared barn and across the adjoining field. What he saw when he topped the hill caused him to put his hands on his knees, both of which were trembling.

The Schwartz family was huddled near a tree in the middle of their front yard.

A fire truck with its sirens blaring and lights flashing was barreling down the lane.

Fire was rapidly devouring the house, but at least everyone was out.

Homes could be rebuilt. That thought circled round and round his brain as he ran toward Becca's family. He was nearly on top of them before he realized they were all staring toward the house. Francine and Georgia were crying. Hannah and Isabelle stood close together holding hands. Sarah was pleading with her boys not to rush back into the house.

"Your *dat* went. He'll find her."

He didn't have to ask who. Instead, he turned and ran toward the burning building. He was nearly to the porch when Samuel tumbled out of the house, a blanket wrapped around Becca, both of them gasping for breath.

Instead of asking questions, he supported Becca on the other side and helped walk her to her family. He wanted to pick her up and carry her. He wanted to pull her into his arms and never let her go.

He thought Becca might collapse into her mother's embrace, but instead, she dropped the blanket around her shoulders and ran to her *bruder* Clyde.

"I thought you were in there. Thought you would be trapped because your room has no windows."

"I was with Melinda. We were out late. When I came home, I saw… I saw…" And then he turned and walked away from the group, his head bowed and his shoulders shaking.

"He's okay. He'll be okay." Samuel hurried after Clyde, put his arms around the young man, gave him all of his attention even as the firefighters were climbing out of their truck and the house was collapsing behind him.

"You're okay?" Daniel reached for Becca. He needed to touch her, needed to look in her eyes. "Tell me you're okay. You're not hurt?"

"I'm fine…"

"I was so terrified, Becca. So afraid…" And then he pulled her to him and held her until her shaking lessened.

The firefighters began to spray water from the pump truck onto the perimeter of the fire. There was nothing to be done for the structure, but they made sure that it wouldn't spread to the fields or barn beyond.

Before they'd even finished, neighbors began arriving with blankets and coats and thermoses of hot coffee.

Bishop Saul was one of the first on the scene, speaking with Sarah and Samuel first, then taking a moment with each of the children.

Paramedics arrived and checked out

everyone's breathing, put some salve on Samuel's hands, which had been burned slightly when he went back into the house looking for Becca.

Each of their neighbors—Amish and *Englisch*—came over and shared their condolences, and then they offered clothes, showers, a place to stay. Several times Daniel heard someone proclaim, "A week before Christmas. What a tragedy."

Sarah looked overwhelmed, and her children were traumatized, confused and exhausted. It was the bishop who finally stepped in.

"The firefighters will stay and make sure there are no flare-ups."

He was interrupted by an older gentleman wearing a firefighter's uniform. "We won't know the cause for certain until the blaze is completely out and we can sift through the wreckage. Did you have a wood-burning stove in the middle of the house?"

"Ya." Samuel's voice was shaky. "In the sitting room."

"The fire appeared to be hottest there. My guess is it started in the stove pipe." He pulled off his helmet and wiped a beefy hand over his face. "Can't tell you how glad I am you had those fire alarms installed. I'm aware some Amish don't, but tonight, they saved your lives."

"Gotte saved our lives," Samuel said.

"Perhaps *Gotte* provided the smoke alarms." Bishop Saul thanked the fireman, then turned back to the family. "Where were we?"

"You were telling us what's been done."

"Oh, yes. The Bontragers have taken your gelding to their place for now. I suggest that you all come to my house. We'll feed the children, have some coffee and figure out what to do next."

"We'll never all fit in your buggy," Samuel pointed out.

Which was the opening that Daniel had been waiting for. "I'll run and fetch mine."

"That would be very kind, Daniel. Thank you, and thank you for staying with my family through this night."

Had the night ended?

Was that the pale light of dawn at the edge of the eastern horizon?

He had no idea, and it didn't matter. What mattered was that Becca was okay and none of her family had been injured. Daniel wasn't ready to let any of them out of his sight.

He jogged back to his house, paused to grab his hat and coat, then harnessed Constance, who looked rather surprised to be going somewhere so close to dawn.

Within the hour they'd loaded the entire family up and traveled the short distance to the bishop's home. They walked inside to find three of the women from their district there. They'd already made coffee and set out milk and juice for the children. The kitchen cabinets were covered with breakfast casseroles, breads and fruit salads.

The room was full to overflowing, but when Saul raised his hands, everyone quieted. Though he didn't bow his head, Daniel understood that he was offering a prayer on their behalf.

"We are grateful, this day, for the well-being of this family—our *bruders* and *schweschdern*. We are grateful to you, *Gotte*, that you have provided, even as our hearts grieve for what is lost. We are grateful for one another."

Amens filled the room, then everyone was filling their plate and talking about the events of the night.

Becca took her plate to a corner of the living room, and Daniel thought maybe she wanted to be alone. Then she looked up, right at him, and it was as if he could hear her thoughts.

He crossed the room in four long strides and sat on the floor beside her.

"Are you okay?"

"You already asked me that."

"But are you?"

"*Ya.* I am." She stared at her plate, then set it on the floor and covered her face with her hands.

"Talk to me, Becca."

"I had a…a dream, and then when I woke and realized what was happening, I was so afraid."

"Anyone would have been."

"Even as it was happening, I thought, *This will be okay. We know what to do. We're okay.*"

"I'm so grateful you were."

"But then I remembered Clyde. Clyde, who snores so loud that I can sometimes hear him through the walls. He sleeps so hard that he once slept through an entire train ride to Ohio to see our cousins— whistle stops and conductors and passengers jostling back and forth." She crossed her arms around her middle, no longer trying to hide the tears streaming down her face. "I was terrified that he hadn't heard the alarms, that he'd sleep through the fire. That he'd die because he wouldn't wake up. I've never been that afraid."

Daniel understood that there was nothing he could say to that, nothing he needed to say. So instead, he pulled her into his arms and let her weep.

Someone was sent to tell Abigail that they were fine. Since she was in her final month of pregnancy, they didn't want her to hear of the fire and worry for even one second.

The next hour passed with everyone eating their fill. Eventually the neighbors who had prepared the breakfast left, and the bishop finally called a meeting in the kitchen.

Becca and her *mamm* and *dat* filed back into the kitchen. Saul and Sarah and Samuel sat, but Becca remained standing, so Daniel did, as well.

Daniel glanced from Samuel to Becca, then back again. "If you'd like me to go…"

"*Nein.* It's *gut* for you to be here." Samuel placed his hand over his wife's.

Saul cleared his throat. "We will rebuild your home, of course. There's plenty of money in the benevolence fund, so there won't need to be an auction." Saul glanced at Daniel, held his gaze for a moment.

Daniel had the slightest fear that Saul would spill his secret, but instead, the bishop nodded and continued.

"Unfortunately it looks like we're in for some wintry weather the next few weeks, so it will be past the first of the year before we can get started."

"However long it takes," Samuel said. "We appreciate it. We really do."

"You have done the same for others, Samuel. Your appreciation is noted, but don't start thinking that you owe anyone. You do not. You are an important part of our community, and as such, we support one another. Am I clear?"

"*Ya.*"

"*Gut.* Now the more immediate problem is where you're to live until the house is rebuilt. *Gotte* has blessed you with a big family. We've had several come forward already and offer a spare room."

"We'll have to be split up..." Understanding dawned on Sarah's face. She looked up at her husband, and Samuel shrugged.

"If it's the only way."

"It'll only be a few weeks." Saul tapped the table. "We'll begin rebuilding as soon as the weather allows."

Daniel didn't think about what he said next. If he had, he would have realized that it was a selfish thing—wanting the entire Schwartz family near him, wanting Becca near him. They'd become such an integral part of his life. He couldn't stand to see them farmed out, not even for a few weeks.

But all of that occurred to him later.

At the moment, he didn't bother analyzing what he was about to do. Instead, he stepped forward and said what was on his heart. "*Nein*, you don't have to break up the family. You can all stay with me."

Chapter Eleven

Becca, her parents and the bishop all turned to stare at Daniel. It was Saul who found his voice first. "You're saying that you'd take the *entire* family into your home?"

Mamm had closed her eyes, clasped her hands together and was uttering a prayer of relief. *Dat*, for once, seemed speechless, and Becca couldn't believe that she'd heard Daniel correctly. It was one thing to offer sympathy for a neighbor, another thing entirely to change your life for them.

"Why's everyone looking at me as if I suggested something outrageous?"

"Because our family can be a lot." Becca glanced into the bishop's sitting room. All seven of her younger siblings were piled on the couch—Hannah on Clyde's lap, Isabelle on David's. Eli, Francine and Georgia were squished in next to them—as if they needed to be close, needed to be certain that the entire family was intact. "They're quiet now because they're still in shock, but you're talking about allowing ten people to move in with you."

"I can count. I certainly don't want to argue, but I also don't see what the big deal is. You are my neighbors. You're my closest friends in Shipshe. Why should your family be separated if they don't have to be?" He stared up at the ceiling for a moment, then added somewhat defiantly, "There's plenty of room."

Saul looked to Samuel, waiting for him to decide. But Samuel had already made his decision, Becca could tell that as plain as day. From the tears in his eyes to the way he clasped her *mamm*'s hand, it was obvious that he would accept. He stood, stepped toward Daniel, placed a hand on his shoulder and tried to speak. He cleared his throat twice, as if he could dislodge the sorrow there, and then swiped a hand across his eyes.

Seeing that—seeing her *dat*, who always had a handy joke to tell and a smile on his face, break down—undid her more than even the sight of their family home in flames. She felt the tears slip down her cheeks and was afraid she might break into giant sobs. The exhaustion of all that had happened felt like a heavy blanket that threatened to weigh her down.

"A friend is never truly known until a man has a need. This day my family had a need, and you have stepped forward to fill it. *Danki*, Daniel. We accept, and we thank you with all our hearts."

Samuel pulled Daniel into a hug. Becca looked up in time to catch the expression on Daniel's face, the way his eyes closed and the sigh escaped his lips, as if he were the one setting down a giant burden—and perhaps he was. Maybe *Gotte* was using this tragedy to heal Daniel in ways that Becca couldn't completely understand.

Samuel turned to Sarah and slipped his hand in hers. "Let's go tell the *kinder*."

Before she followed her husband into the other room, Sarah walked over to Daniel, stood on tiptoe and kissed him on the cheek.

Saul smiled and said, "It's settled, then." With a wink, he turned and followed Becca's parents into the sitting room.

Daniel looked as if he was afraid Becca might burst into tears again. She didn't. She squared her shoulders, wiped her cheeks dry and sank into a kitchen chair. "I hope you know what you're doing."

"It's not that big a deal, Becca."

"You moved here to be alone."

"It's not as if your family is going to live with me forever."

"Might seem that way, though." She tried to smile to soften the words, but it felt as if she were stretching her lips in an awkward angle.

"Your family isn't that bad."

"Oh, don't misunderstand me. I love them. And I appreciate what you're doing." She stared at the table, tracing the swirls in the wood with her fingertips. "Living with Hannah and Isabelle is like living with twin tornadoes. Clyde rarely remembers to wipe his feet. David eats more than a single person should be able to, and Eli has an old harmonica that he has taken to playing at odd hours in the barn."

Daniel sat down next to her, reached forward and thumbed a smudge of soot off her face.

"David is hardly around at all—just long enough to eat and leave dirty laundry tossed about."

"What about Francine and Georgia? Aren't you going to warn me about them?"

"Georgia's all right—though you'll trip over her because she's plopped down somewhere to read a book. Francine is still insisting she's begun her *rumspringa*, though we all keep telling her she's not old enough."

"And your parents?"

"*Mamm* will be cooking all the time. You'll probably put on ten pounds."

"Are you saying I'll get fat?"

"As for *Dat*, you know how it is with his jokes, he seems to have an endless supply."

"Anything else?"

"Only all my projects…" The horror of what they'd been through hit her then. She pressed her fingers to her lips, closed her eyes and tried to calm her emotions. Her heart had other ideas. It tripped and rattled and seemed to push against her rib cage.

She felt as if her heart was going to collapse and explode all at the same time.

She felt as if the world was simply too much.

Daniel stood and pulled her into his arms, and Becca allowed herself to stop being the strong one. For the first time since smelling smoke, she allowed the fear and sorrow to have its way. She wept for all that they'd lost, for the terror she'd felt when she thought Clyde was trapped inside, for the anguish of seeing the home she'd grown up in disappear in flames.

Daniel didn't try to reason with her.

He didn't point out that everything would be okay or that they had much to be thankful for. He held her and let her weep. It was during that moment of intense grief both felt and shared that Becca accepted what she'd probably known for a long time—that she'd fallen in love with Daniel Glick.

The rest of the day passed in a blur of activity. By the time they reached Daniel's house, Bishop Saul had already put out the word. Hour after hour, people from their church as well as *Englischers* from the community showed up with clothes, bedding, mattresses, even extra food.

"Early Christmas," Daniel muttered as

he stuffed yet another casserole into his refrigerator.

Christmas was ten days away. Becca didn't want to think about it. The few gifts she and her *mamm* had made had been destroyed in the fire. Instead of dwelling on that, she said, "I warned you about the ten pounds, and *Mamm* hasn't even started cooking yet."

Dinner was a somber affair, owing to the fact that nearly everyone was falling asleep in the chicken soup that Abigail had brought over. It was hard to believe that her baby was due before the end of the month.

At least the impending birth gave everyone something to look forward to.

If Becca thought about it too hard, the winter stretched in front of them like an endless parade of cold days, days she would be forced to stay inside, days in close proximity to Daniel, whom she had such strong feelings for. She didn't completely understand those feelings yet. She couldn't even flee to the barn for private time, since it was his barn as well as theirs.

She'd just have to put a lid on her feelings. Daniel couldn't have been more clear about where he stood. How many times had he said that he wasn't looking for a *fraa*? Every time one of the unmarried women at church threw a look his way, he practically ran for a rabbit hole.

She believed he did care for her, but she also understood that he had no intention to marry anytime soon. When she thought about it in that light, she convinced herself that his feelings for her were not serious. There had been a few kisses, but now it seemed as if those lighthearted moments had happened a hundred years ago. As for his comforting her earlier in Bishop Saul's home, no doubt he'd been doing just that—comforting a friend who had just lost their home.

No, she would not be confessing her feelings to Daniel.

Her heart had endured quite enough for one day.

Throughout the meal, she'd steal a glimpse at him, prepared to see a look of regret on his face. Surely he was beginning to understand the enormity of what he'd done by inviting the entire family into his home. If he was regretting it, then he was hiding it well.

He even laughed at her *dat*'s joke.

"What do you call a horse that lives next door?" Samuel barely waited before delivering his punch line: "A neigh-bor."

Hannah and Daniel were the only ones to laugh aloud.

Isabelle, attempting to butter her piece of corn bread, said, "Our horse will live here now. Right? Since the Bontragers brought him back? I wonder if Old Boy is scared, being in a different place and all."

Becca guessed that everyone at the table understood Isabelle wasn't speaking only of the horse. It was Daniel who suggested checking on the animals. "We can go out together, maybe take both Old Boy and Constance a carrot."

"I wanna go, too." Hannah moved her spoon around in her soup. "Maybe I can take them my peas. *Mamm*, do I have to eat these peas?"

Which turned the conversation to all the food that had been donated, how generous their neighbors had been—both *Englisch* and Amish. Daniel met Becca's gaze and winked. Oh, but he was a charmer when he wanted to be.

By nine that evening, everyone was in bed. They'd found a place for each person to sleep, barely. The five girls managed to fit into one room with a bit of creative rearranging. Clyde, David and Eli spread across the living room, and it wasn't lost on Becca that Eli was using Daniel's sleeping bag—the same sleeping bag he'd once slept in on the back porch.

Well, at least no one was in the barn. Her parents took the smallest guest bedroom, claiming there were only two of them, so they didn't need as much space. Daniel tried to give up his room, but everyone put up such a fuss that he raised his hands in surrender.

Becca lay on the mattress she was sharing with Hannah and Isabelle and listened as her *schweschdern*'s breathing slowed. Why couldn't she fall asleep? Shouldn't she be exhausted? But there were too many images flipping through her brain—rushing through the smoke, flames shooting out of the top of her house, Daniel standing in the cold with her siblings, her family huddled together as the firefighters worked to contain the blaze.

She tried deep breathing, praying, even counting sheep. Finally she stood, reached for her robe and tiptoed out of the room. If she'd been afraid of waking her *bruders*, that thought evaporated when she slipped through the living room. They were all snoring loudly.

Once in the kitchen, she pulled the pocket door closed, turned the switch on the battery lantern Daniel kept on the counter and set about making herself a cup of tea. Filling the kettle with water, setting it on the stove, putting the tea bag into a mug—all of those things were such normal, ordinary things to do that they calmed her nerves and quieted her thoughts. Her stomach growled, reminding her that she'd eaten very little at dinner. She foraged through the pantry and came away with a container full of oatmeal bites. She inhaled deeply of her best friend's baking—no one made oatmeal cookies like Liza, and the miniature ones were the absolute best. Just last week, Becca had joked that they were tiny bites of goodness, sprinkled with sugar.

She stood there in the pantry, holding the container, smelling their goodness and letting the trauma of the past twenty-four hours slip off her shoulders. Of course, it was at that moment that Daniel appeared.

"They taste even better than they smell."

"Oh! You scared a year off my life."

Instead of answering that, he reached around her, plucked a cookie from the container and popped it in his mouth.

"Water's still hot if you'd like some tea."

Which was how they found themselves huddled on the far side of the table, the lantern turned to low, eating cookies late at night.

Daniel kept thinking about how he felt when he'd put his arms around Becca. He'd experienced an overwhelming sense of having finally come home, as if after a long and tedious journey he'd found where he belonged. Could holding a person represent so much?

It had been so hard to watch her struggle all day, harder even than watching the fire devour her family's home. As far as opening his house to her family, how could he not?

They'd welcomed him when they knew nothing about him.

They'd taken care of him when he was sick.

And the entire community had helped to rebuild his home.

He liked to think he would have made the same offer to anyone in need, but he was honest enough with himself to realize that Becca had claimed a special place in his heart. He thought maybe she felt the same way about him.

But would she if she knew the truth?

If she knew who he really was, would she still care for him? He wasn't willing to risk it. Not yet, anyway. Maybe in a year or two, when she had a chance to know him better.

"You're awfully quiet." She studied him over the top of her mug.

"Can't gather my thoughts with the sounds of three trains in my living room."

"*Ya*, my *bruders* snore quite loud. Are you having regrets about inviting us here?"

"Not at all." He reached for another

cookie, allowed his hand to brush against hers, and looked up to see her blushing in the glow of the lamplight.

"How are you holding up…really?"

"My mind won't stop spinning."

"I can imagine."

"I keep seeing the smoke, and then it's as if I re-experience the fear that my family might be inside the burning house. My heart starts racing and my palms start sweating…" She shook her head. "I sound crazy."

"Not at all. You've been through quite a trauma, Becca. Give yourself some time to process all that has happened."

"I was so scared."

"Scared is what praying's for."

She'd been staring at the table, but at his words, her head popped up. "I thought praying only when you're in need was… you know…bad."

"Is that the only time you pray?"

"Nein."

He studied the cookie he'd retrieved,

then pushed it across the table to her. She picked it up and nibbled around the edges.

"I don't think *Gotte* minds that we cry out to him when we're afraid. Didn't Job do the same thing? And Jonas? And Abraham? You're in *gut* company if you pray when you're scared."

"When did you get so wise?"

"Didn't say I was."

"It's because of all those things you jot down in your journal."

"Notebook."

"Whatever."

Daniel sat back, feeling on more solid ground when they were teasing one another. "I know I probably don't know what I think I do..."

"You lost me."

"Well, all that stuff I write...it makes sense to me when I jot it down, but it doesn't mean that I'm wise or anything. Only that..." He shook his head, unwilling or unable to go on. He wasn't sure which.

"Only that what, Daniel?" She leaned

closer, stared up into his eyes, and Daniel fell a little bit further in love.

"Um, only that…" What had they been talking about? His notebook and truth and life. "Only that it seems some of it you can learn that way, by paying attention, I mean."

"Hmm." Becca sat back and sipped her nearly cold tea. "I guess. Life is hard."

"That it is."

"I thought it was hard before, when we were poor. Now we're homeless and poor, so you know… I realize life wasn't so hard yesterday."

"The bishop is already scheduling a workday to rebuild."

"I know he is, and I know I'm lucky to be Amish. If I was *Englisch*, I'd have to wait for an insurance check, then a contractor…" She gave a mock shudder.

"How do you know so much about *Englisch* ways?"

"Look around you. Half our neighbors are *Englisch*. Half the boxes of stuff people brought today are from the *Englisch*. They're *gut* people, only different in the way they choose to live their lives."

"I guess." He turned his mug left, then right, thinking of his *bruder*. Finally he raised his eyes to hers. "Have you ever thought of leaving…"

"Shipshe?"

"*Nein*. Our faith. Have you ever thought of not being Amish?"

"Maybe once, when I was a *youngie*. Younger than Georgia is now. When I was nine years old I'd read this book about a girl who was an Olympic gymnast, and I thought that would be an awesome thing to become."

"A gymnast?"

"Don't look at me that way. I could do a mean cartwheel." She stared across the room, no doubt seeing another place and another time. "I asked *Mamm* about it, and she explained that Amish don't seek recognition on a world stage. She reminded me that we strive to be humble and set apart."

"And how did the nine-year-old Becca respond to that?"

"I took my school bag, stuffed my extra dress, *kapp* and pillow in it, and trudged off down the road."

"You didn't." Yet somehow he could picture this. Apparently, she'd been full of spunk even then.

"I did. Made it to the mailbox, took a left, then another right, and then suddenly I was lost."

"You hadn't gone far?"

"*Nein*. Only over to where Abigail is now, but it seemed farther. I was so afraid and I sat down on this rock. I sat down and hoped someone I knew would walk by."

"And did they?"

"*Ya*. My *onkel* Jeremiah. He asked me what I was doing, I told him that I was running away to be an Olympic gymnast, and he said maybe I should go home for dinner, then start out early the next day."

"Smart guy."

"Exactly. By the time he'd walked me home, I was so happy to see our house that I ran into my *mamm*'s arms and told her I'd missed her." Becca closed her right hand into a fist, rubbed it against her heart. "*Mamm* told me years later that I'd only been gone an hour, that she thought I was out playing in the barn."

"That's a *gut* story."

"I think that's when I understood what home meant—that it was a safe place with people who love me." She laughed, a soft delicate sound. "It was the only time I thought I might like to not be Amish. This life is what I know, and it's who I am. Does that make sense?"

"It does to me."

She'd leaned forward, and Daniel could no more have stopped himself than he could have stopped water flowing from the sea. He pushed their cups out of the way, framed her face in his hands and brought his lips gently to hers.

He kissed her once, and then again.

With her eyes closed, she put her hands on top of his, and Daniel almost groaned. Wait a year to tell her how he felt? How was he going to be able to do that? He wanted to ask Becca to marry him now. He wanted to bare his soul, explain his past, beg her forgiveness for all the half-truths he'd told.

Becca squeezed his hands, stood and whispered good-night.

Leaving Daniel sitting in his own kitchen, wondering how his world had managed to turn into something that he didn't even recognize.

Chapter Twelve

Daniel could barely understand what had happened to his barn or buggy or home.

All that he owned had been taken over by Christmas elves—mainly in the persons of Hannah and Isabelle, though he suspected they had help. Holly sprigs decorated every windowsill, as did small battery-operated candles. Red berries that the boys had found along the Pumpkinvine Trail adorned the fireplace hearth and the center of the kitchen table.

Though the Schwartz family had escaped their fire with only the clothes on their backs, still there were secret meetings, newspapers disappearing to reappear later wrapped around mysterious boxes, bright red ribbons on packages that were hidden behind couches, in the pantry, even under his bed.

How did a box large enough to hold a man-size coat appear under his bed?

He left it there, shaking his head and telling himself that in only two more days the craziness would stop.

He had a strong feeling that his life would never return to what it had been before, and he found that thought didn't bother him as much as it might have a year or even a month ago. Becca and her family had only been in his home a week, but already their routines were precious to him.

Samuel's jokes as they ate each meal around the table.

Clyde's muddy boots leaving trails from the mudroom to the kitchen and back again.

David's appetite, which was indeed quite amazing.

Georgia's stack of books—where did she get them all? Some were stamped Shipshewana Public Library; others were quite worn around the edges.

Francine's *Englisch* blue jeans and hoodie that she thought no one knew about.

He'd even grown used to the plaintive sound of Eli's harmonica as he did a final walk-through of the horses—always with Hannah and Isabelle trailing next to him.

His life was fuller, richer than it had ever been, and Daniel realized with a start that he was happy. He hadn't been this unburdened since...since his family had inherited the money.

What a curse that blessing had turned out to be.

Only it wasn't the money that had been the problem. He understood that now. His family had been waiting to fall apart at the seams. The money had just caused that disintegration to happen a little faster than it might have otherwise.

He walked from his bedroom through the kitchen. A new drawing sat on the table—the girls left him one nearly every day. This one had two stick horses with extraordinarily large heads. One was labeled *Ol Boy* and the other *Constant*. He smiled at the misspellings, but what tugged at his heart was the stick-figure man standing in between them. He had arms twice as long as his legs, a pear-shaped head wearing an Amish hat, and on his shirt was a big heart, instead of a pocket. In case he didn't recognize himself, someone had penciled the word *Daneel* underneath.

Becca's *mamm* walked into the room and caught him staring at the picture. "The girls left that for you."

"*Ya*. Their penmanship is improving."

"Can't say the same for their spelling, but in this case, I suppose it's the thought that counts."

"Indeed."

She patted him on the shoulder as she

passed him by, but must have seen something in his eyes, because instead of continuing to the stove she backed up. "Is everything okay?"

"*Ya*. It's fine."

That was another thing. Though Sarah never seemed to stop working, nothing slipped past her. She was the first to bandage a scratched knee, find a misplaced *kapp* or counsel a bruised heart.

"You looked a bit sad, there, for a minute."

"Thinking of my family, I guess." The admission surprised him, but Sarah only nodded her head in understanding.

"I don't know the details, and I don't need to, but I pray for you and for them every night."

She left it there, not expecting or needing an explanation. Daniel wondered at the simple way she cared for her family, even as he hurried outside to be sure both horses were hitched up and ready to go. By the time he walked back into the kitchen, everyone had gathered at the table and a steaming bowl of chicken soup was at each place.

He scooted into his normal seat at the end of the bench, and each member of the family bowed their head to pray.

It occurred to Daniel then that Christmas was about so much more than gifts hidden under the bed. This family had no money to speak of, yet they were filled with joy—for each other, for the gifts they'd made, for the Christ child. As he helped Isabelle take a pat of butter for her bread and then pass the dish on, he realized that he was actually looking forward to the school play they were about to attend and the festivities of the next few days.

How long had it been since he'd felt anything but sadness and remorse on the holidays?

But this year was different.

This year he was surrounded by *frein-*

den, and he was sitting across from the girl he hoped to marry.

Becca glanced up, caught him staring and immediately reached for her napkin, which only made him smile wider.

It wasn't food on her face that made him stare, it was what she'd come to mean to him—and he meant to find a private moment to tell her before the Christmas holiday had passed.

They fitted into two buggies, though it was a bit snug. He still didn't understand how the Schwartz family had ever managed with only one. He couldn't help reaching for Becca's hand and squeezing it, which was immediately noticed by Hannah.

"Are you going to kiss her?"

"Hannah, that's rude."

Daniel turned to smile at Georgia, who was pushing up her glasses and tugging Hannah back onto the rear seat bench.

"Why was it rude? I'm just asking a question."

"And we saw them kissing yesterday in the barn." Isabelle piped in. "So it's natural to wonder."

"Still, it's private. How about we play a game of I Spy?"

Daniel started to laugh. Becca shook her head, but she didn't pull her hand away. "Those two are a handful."

"So you've mentioned."

The schoolhouse was decorated in snowflakes cut from local newspapers, construction paper formed into chains of garland, and pine cones decorated with glitter. Apparently, whoever had been in charge of the glitter had been a bit overzealous, as the stuff seemed to be everywhere—on the floor, in the seats, and even a bit on the ceiling, Daniel looked up and saw. How did glitter land on the ceiling?

With five of the Schwartz children still in school, there was at least one member of the family in every skit, song and recitation. The punch and cookies afterward were especially good, but Daniel's mind was on something else. When was he going to ask Becca to marry him? Where could he possibly do it? Finding a single private moment wasn't easy. Finding several private moments was almost impossible.

Becca stepped closer and put a hand on his arm. "We can go if you want."

"Oh, okay. Sure. Where...?"

"They've all gone."

"Who has all gone?"

"My family."

"I don't understand."

She raised her eyes to his as a light blush splashed across her cheeks. "They already went home, is what I'm saying—home to your house."

"All in your *dat*'s buggy?"

"*Ya*. I mean, I think Clyde and David and Francine left with *freinden*, but *Mamm* took the younger ones home."

"Oh."

"They thought we might like to be alone."

A moment alone was exactly what Daniel had been wishing for, so perhaps this was a little push for him to do what he'd been wanting to do for nearly a week now. He wasn't one to dawdle once he'd made up his mind, and he had definitely made up his mind that he was in love with Becca Schwartz.

Once they were in the buggy—alone—he couldn't think of where to go.

"Would you like to drive to town and get a piece of pie or something?"

"*Nein*. I'm full. Unless you're hungry…"

"I'm full, too." He called out to Constance, but when he reached the road, he didn't know which direction to go. His brain felt a little addled, like when he woke up after a particularly deep sleep.

"Perhaps we could drive around and look at Christmas lights for a little while."

"*Ya*. That's a *gut* idea."

"Constance seems to like the snow."

"She likes to go—doesn't matter if it's

sunny, raining or snowing. She's sort of like Hannah and Isabelle."

There was a light dusting of snow on the fields, not enough to affect the roads, but enough to give the landscape a nice Christmastime feel. *Englisch* houses sported inflatable yard decorations and large light displays. Amish homes were easily recognizable by candles in the window. He drove slowly through the streets of Shipshe. Becca chatted about the school festivities, the Christmas displays, and how much she was looking forward to Christmas Day. But Daniel barely heard what she was saying. He was growing more and more nervous by the minute.

His hands had begun to sweat, and twice he'd dropped the horse's reins.

"Are you cold?"

"*Nein*. This blanket is warm, and your heater works well." She sighed. "*Dat* would love to have a heater in our buggy. *Mamm* would, too, though she'd never ask for one."

"Your *mamm* isn't one to complain."

"No, she's not."

A familiar look came over Becca's face then, and he knew that she was planning another scheme, another way to pull her family out of poverty. Only she didn't need another scheme. She had him. She just didn't know it yet.

So he drove to the city park, where the trees had been decorated with tiny white lights. Fortunately they had the place almost to themselves—a church van full of youth was loading up to leave on the far side of the parking lot, and an older couple had parked their truck and were walking hand in hand down the path.

Now was the time.

Now was when he needed to tell Becca how he felt.

He directed Constance beneath the boughs of a fir tree and set the brake. He then turned to the woman he'd grown to love and covered her hands with his.

"There's something I want to talk to you about."

"There is?" Her eyes widened, not in surprise so much as anticipation. She couldn't be surprised, could she? Surely she understood how he felt.

He swallowed around the lump in his throat. "I care about you, Becca."

"You do?"

"Ya." He nodded his head, feeling like an idiot. Why couldn't he just spit it out? "In fact, I love you, and I want to marry you."

She stared at him a moment, then leaned forward and kissed him gently on the lips. "I care about you, too, Daniel. I do. You're a kind man with a generous heart, but…"

"But?" He hadn't expected a *but*.

"But I don't really know anything about you."

"Oh." Daniel couldn't form a cohesive thought. He'd been so keyed up about asking that he hadn't considered what he'd say next. Yet here Becca was, waiting for his answer.

"Um. You don't know anything about me?"

"Not about your past, not really, and I understand that. I do. After our talk. You remember, the talk that you gave me when you caught me snooping?"

He nodded, trying to focus on what she was saying and not the sweetness of her smile or the pinkness of her lips.

"You told me a little then, like about your *bruder* leaving the faith. But you said...what was it? That you didn't want to go into your past—*not now, maybe not ever.*"

He winced at the words.

"Which is fine for *freinden*, Daniel. But if I agree to marry you, to be your *fraa*, then I need to know your past every bit as much as you need to know mine."

She sat back, hands folded in her lap, watching him.

When had Becca become the wise one?

And why was he hesitating to tell her everything?

He cleared his throat. "You're right. There should be no secrets between us."

"Exactly."

"And I know I can trust you with the details of my past."

"Of course."

"Only it's hard." He stared out at Constance. The horse didn't seem bothered by the cold evening or the light snow. For all he knew, she was enjoying looking at the lights. He understood as much about the thoughts of horses as he did about the thoughts of women—make that one woman.

"It's hard to talk about a thing after you've stayed silent for so long." He turned his complete attention toward Becca. He knew he needed to look her straight in the eyes when he told her about his past. "I'm a millionaire."

"Excuse me?"

"I inherited a large sum of money when

I turned twenty-five, we all did. That is, everyone in my family did."

Becca had sat up straighter and was looking at him as if he'd sprouted ears out of the top of his head. "Is this a joke?"

"*Nein.* Listen to me. Becca..." He reached for her hand, pulled it toward him and stared at it as he traced his thumb over her palm. "My *mamm*'s *bruder* was Mennonite. I barely remember the man. Only met him a few times. He was *gut* at writing code for computers—"

"Code?"

"And he developed some app, something *Englischers* use on their phones. He sold it and made a lot of money, and then some big corporation used his code for their apps. The entire thing snowballed. Apparently, it surprised even him, and I don't pretend to understand it all."

"You're a millionaire?"

She wasn't smiling. She didn't look thrilled about this revelation. In fact, she looked as if she'd been chiseled from ice.

"Each member of my family inherited a portion of the money. We receive it when we turn twenty-five, and even then we only receive so much a year, or I might give it all away. I suppose my *onkel* knew we might do that. He understood the Amish life. I guess that's why he set it up the way he did, where we receive a certain percentage each year."

"A million dollars?"

"A little more than that." From the look on her face, he was pretty sure he shouldn't tell her just how much more, not right now. Perhaps the entire revelation had been too much. Maybe he should have broken the news more gently. But how?

"It's why my parents fight all the time, why my *bruder* left the faith, and why even my *schweschdern* seem so...changed."

"Is this why you broke off your relationship with the girl you were to marry?"

"I found out she didn't care for me at all...only for my money." He was once again surprised that the memory of Sheila no longer felt like a knife in his heart.

"So you moved here and pretended to be poor?"

"Well, yes, but no. It wasn't like that."

"Were you laughing at us this entire time?"

"*Nein.* Of course not."

"Our simple meals and our plain clothes and… No wonder you made such a big deal about our single buggy. You and your fancy horse."

"I can explain about the horse." She was staring at him with such disbelief that he found himself stumbling over his words. "I didn't want the money. Didn't want to live that way anymore, but then, when I got here, I knew that it would be a waste of money to purchase an older horse."

"Like ours?"

"I reasoned that a horse was something I'd be using for the next twenty years. I could live in a dilapidated house on a run-down farm, but when I saw Constance I knew that I—"

"Take me home."

"What?"

"You heard me. I want to go home right now."

"Becca, you're taking this all wrong."

"You have been lying to me since the day you arrived—me, my family, our community. You've been pretending to be just like us when in fact you were sitting back and laughing."

"I never laughed at you." He felt his temper rise, knew that he needed to shut his mouth or he was going to say something that he'd regret.

"Take me home, please."

"I thought you cared about me."

"And I thought I knew you." If she'd shouted the words at him, they wouldn't have hurt nearly as much. But the look on her face, the expression of disappointment, tore at his heart.

They rode home in silence.

Daniel tried to figure out where he'd gone wrong. How had this evening turned so horribly bad? How should he have handled it? But he knew the answer to that. He should have been honest from the beginning.

Still, he had to try one more time. As he directed Constance into his lane, he glanced Becca's way, but she wouldn't look at him.

"Becca, this doesn't have to be a bad thing. You care for me. I know you do, and I care for you. The money, well, it could be a good thing. It could help your family."

"I don't need you to rescue me, Daniel." Her chin rose a fraction of an inch. "I don't need your money. My family doesn't need your money. What we needed was your friendship—and friends don't lie to one another. They don't pretend to be something that they're not."

He'd barely stopped the buggy when she jumped out and fled up the porch steps.

* * *

The next twenty-four hours felt like an eternity to Becca. She avoided Daniel whenever possible, which wasn't easy given the amount of snow falling outside and the amount of people inside.

Their family tradition was to spend Christmas Eve with only the immediate family, but this year that included Daniel. It would have been strange to leave him out, given they were living in his house.

Though her heart felt bruised, she couldn't help seeing what was happening around her.

Daniel helping her *mamm* slice the chocolate cake.

Daniel playing chess with Eli.

Daniel sitting with Hannah and Isabelle and reading to them.

When her father told a Christmas joke—*What do sheep say to each other at Christmas? Merry Christmas to ewe*—Daniel laughed.

When Georgia misplaced her book, Daniel helped her find it.

And when Clyde fell despondent because he couldn't walk to his girlfriend's in the snowstorm, it was Daniel who told him to take his buggy.

The truth was that he cared about her family.

That wasn't fake.

That wasn't a lie.

It was an uncomfortable truth—uncomfortable because it made her question whether he cared for her. It seemed as if he did, but then, why had he lied to her for so long?

It was after she helped to clean the dinner dishes, finished the last preparations for the next day's celebration, and tucked Isabelle and Hannah into bed that her *mamm* tugged on her arm and suggested they walk to the barn together.

Becca walked straight to the stall that now held all of her chickens. Carl-the-bad-tempered-rooster was sitting on top of the chicken house they'd built. The hens peeked out from their nests. She didn't believe for a minute that her wayward rooster had changed his stripes, but she was grateful that for this one evening he'd chosen to behave.

Becca made her way to Old Boy's stall, intent on giving him all the carrots in her pockets. Then Constance stuck her head over the door, nudging her arm, and she couldn't help laughing. It was ridiculous to be angry with the horse. It wasn't the mare's fault that her owner was dishonest.

Her *mamm* stepped in front of Old Boy's stall, cooing to him and scratching him between the ears.

That image—of her mother so completely satisfied with life—caused Becca's tears to flow freely. She tried to swipe at them casually, but little passed her mother's notice.

"Want to talk about it?"

"I don't know."

"Okay. So start, and if you change your mind, you can stop."

"You make it sound so easy."

"There's nothing easy about being hurt, Becca. Now tell me what happened."

So, she did. She confessed her feelings for Daniel, his feelings for her, his proposal the evening before and what seemed to her to be this insurmountable thing between them.

"Let me see if I have this straight. You're angry because he's rich and he didn't tell you that from day one."

"Not day one. I'm not naive. I know you don't share those sorts of details with just anyone. But *Mamm*, he knew our family's situation…"

Becca stopped talking when her *mamm* began shaking her head. "Let's keep those two things separate for now. It's certainly not Daniel's fault that we have limited resources."

"We're poor. Just call it what it is."

"Do you really think so?" Her *mamm*'s

smile was gentle, but her voice held a tinge of impatience. "Becca, I wish that you didn't struggle with this. I wish I had *gut* advice to give you for every possible problem you will encounter. But I have never wished for a different life. Your *dat* has been a *gut* husband, and I love my family."

"But—"

"There is no *but* on this point. What you insist on seeing as a huge obstacle is no more than an insignificant detail—like the bow on a gift. What counts is the intention behind the gift. What counts in this family is that we care for each other, not whether we can afford a new buggy."

Becca felt appropriately chastised but still confused. "So you don't think he was wrong?"

"Wrong about what?"

"About keeping the truth of his finances a secret. About pretending to be poor. What if…what if he was laughing at us the whole time?"

"Do you think he was?"

"I don't know."

"You do." Her *mamm* stepped closer, waited for her to look up and then repeated her question. "Do you think Daniel was laughing at this family?"

"Nein." She felt miserable admitting it, but also as if a giant burden had been lifted. "I guess I'm a bit sensitive on the subject."

"A bit?" Her *mamm* reached forward and thumbed away her tears, then straightened her *kapp*. "What's really bothering you?"

"I know how to be poor. I've done it all my life, but I have no idea how to be rich." The confession startled her. Was that really what was bothering her? Fear of the unknown? An unknown that she had been chasing for years?

"Then we will pray that *Gotte* grants you wisdom and clarity in this area. One thing I know is that if you agree to marry Daniel, you have to accept all of him, including his past. It's time for you two to grow up and understand that there are some things in life we don't get to choose. Instead, we trust *Gotte*'s design for our life and then do the best we can."

She hooked her arm through Becca's, they said good-night to the horses and rushed back across the snow-filled night to the house.

Becca was relieved that Daniel wasn't waiting for her.

She needed time to think and pray.

Christmas morning dawned with a clear blue sky and sunshine that would probably melt the snow before evening. Hannah and Isabelle were already at the table by the time Becca made it downstairs.

"We're fasting," Hannah declared.

"That means only milk for breakfast." Isabelle sipped hers carefully, then whispered, "Because the baby Jesus didn't have much when He was born."

"*Ya*, and we want to remember that."

"But later we get cake."

"And ham."

"And presents."

Becca ruffled the hair of both girls, remembering Christmases past—the first time she'd understood what it meant to fast, the time her grandparents from Ohio had come to stay with them, the year when the twins were only babes.

Her *mamm* pushed a mug of coffee into her hands, and before she'd drank even half of it all the men came in through the mudroom, stomping their feet and declaring it a perfect Christmas morning.

It was during the reading of the Christmas story that she finally met Daniel's gaze. The entire family was there—even Abigail, Aaron, William and Thomas. Abigail would have her baby in the next few days. She'd have to. There was simply no way she could get any bigger.

It wasn't uncomfortable with all of them crowded into Daniel's living room. It was cozy. It felt good and right that they should be together like this.

Would she want a bigger house?

It wouldn't make a bit of difference. She could see that now. What mattered was that they were together.

"Why did Baby Jesus have to sleep in the barn?" Hannah asked.

Isabelle perked up. She always perked up when she knew an answer. "Because the motel was full."

"Inn," Francine said. "The inn was full."

"What's an inn?"

"It was a place where people stayed when they were away from home—a long time ago." Georgia pushed up her glasses. "The barn must have been cold and a little smelly."

"It's probably true that it wasn't where Mary and Joseph wanted to have their baby." Her *dat* stared down at the open Bible in his lap. "But it wasn't a surprise to God the Father. Listen to what the angels told the shepherds. *Ye shall find the babe wrapped in swaddling clothes, lying in a manger.* It was a divine appointment they had, and the birth of the Christ Child in a manger? That was *Gotte*'s plan all along."

Hannah squirreled her nose. "I'd rather have a divine appointment in a house than in a stinky barn."

"But barns are nice, too." Isabelle clasped her hands in her lap. "When the hay is fresh, and there's that horsey smell. I kinda like barns."

"I think there's more to this story than whether the babe was born in a smelly stall or a clean room." Clyde shifted in his seat.

Watching him, Becca realized that he'd become a man. When had that happened? While she'd been chasing schemes to improve their lot in life, her *bruder* had grown up. She'd missed it. Glancing around the group, she realized she didn't want to miss anything else. She didn't want finances to be her focus. Maybe she could trust her parents to care for them. Maybe they didn't need her help. Maybe *Gotte* had a plan.

"Explain what you mean by that, son."

"It's that there was no pretense. Can't go much lower than a barn. I think the point might be that we can all approach the Christ child, we can all approach the Lord, without worrying about our status in life."

"Oh, come let us adore Him," Daniel said.

Which started the twins singing, and soon they all joined in. It was a precious moment, one that didn't last nearly long enough. Becca thought that perhaps when she was very old—if she lived to be very old—she would remember them all crowded into Daniel's sitting room as they sang that age-old hymn.

Daniel searched his memory, trying to recall a Christmas like the one he was experiencing, but he couldn't. His family had never had the kind of peace he saw in the faces around him. He was sure that on one level his family did love each other, but there had always been friction between them. The money they'd inherited had only intensified those feelings.

After their Scripture reading, everyone drifted off to various spots. The next few hours passed in a sweet atmosphere of quiet and contemplation. He read his Bible, wrote in his notebook, prayed for himself and this family surrounding him, and he prayed for Becca. He asked that *Gotte* would guide them, even as he realized that he'd lost his heart to her long ago. There was no going back. Regardless of what she decided, he loved and would always love Becca.

He gradually became aware of folks moving around, dishes being heated in the kitchen, laughter and teasing. When he finally walked out of his room, he gasped at the spread on the kitchen table.

"Did you think we were going to eat

sandwiches?" Sarah handed him a platter filled with a giant turkey that she must have cooked the day before. It was stuffed with dressing full of carrots and celery. His stomach growled so loudly that Abigail laughed and nudged him with her elbow. "I'm supposed to have the stomach that draws all the attention."

"I suppose you're ready to have that *boppli*."

"We both are," Aaron admitted. "The rascal wakes us both up in the middle of the night."

Soon they were all gathered around the table, a veritable feast laid out before them. After the blessing, Daniel glanced up and caught Becca watching him. She didn't look away. Didn't blush or smile but simply waited, and Daniel knew what she was waiting for.

He knew what he needed to do.

What he should have done long ago.

So, as the turkey was passed, and the

vegetable dishes were shuffled back and forth, he cleared his throat and dove in.

"There's something I'd like to share with each of you—something I should have shared many weeks ago, but I didn't know how. I suppose I was a little embarrassed. To be truthful, in the past when people learned the truth about me, the result wasn't always *gut*."

He had everyone's attention now, and he didn't want the wonderful meal that Sarah had prepared to go cold, so he got right to the point.

"I'm rich. I inherited a large sum of money a few years ago—my entire family did. It caused quite a bit of strife between everyone. My *bruder* even left the faith, though I hope and pray every day that he will find *Gotte* on whatever path he chooses. That's all beside the point. I'm sorry that I wasn't honest, and I appreciate the way you've made me feel at home here in Shipshewana."

David leaned toward Eli and said in a

mock whisper, "That's how he paid for Constance."

Which started everyone laughing, then the meal proceeded as if he hadn't revealed this long-held secret.

"Why shouldn't you tell a secret on a farm?" Samuel asked. He glanced at Daniel—eyes sparkling and a smile pulling at the corners of his mouth. "Because the potatoes have eyes and the corn has ears."

Groans and laughter echoed around the table.

Even Becca smiled and rolled her eyes. The conversation turned to the meal and gifts and the return to school the following week.

His big revelation hadn't made much of an impression on this group, and that, more than anything else, convinced him that he'd done the right thing.

Now he only had to wait to see if Becca would forgive him.

Chapter Thirteen

After the leftovers had been put away and the dishes washed, they all gathered in the sitting room again. This was one of Becca's favorite moments of Christmas—not because she cared about what gifts she received. She loved watching the expressions of her *bruders* and *schweschdern* as they opened their presents.

Each person pretending to be surprised.

Each person exclaiming over a small thing that was either handmade or cost very little.

Because of the fire, this year they had even less than usual. In fact, they had practically nothing, but somehow everyone had scrambled and managed to come up with gifts.

Hannah and Isabelle received new dolls and new frocks. Both had been donated by members of their church, but they didn't know that. They threw their arms around their *mamm* and thanked her over and over.

Georgia received not one but three new-to-her books.

Francine had taken up knitting, and she received a set of circular needles and a bag of yarn. Becca had stopped by the yarn shop in town hoping to find something on clearance, and the owner had insisted on donating the items. "Fires are terrible things. My parents lost everything in one years ago, and I'll never forget the tragedy of it. The community pulled together, though. That's what they did then, and I think it's what we should still do now."

She wouldn't even consider letting Becca set up a payment plan for the items.

David and Eli received new work tools that they claimed they'd been eyeing for months.

Clyde received buggy blankets for the buggy he hadn't purchased yet. "Glad the money I've managed to save wasn't lost in the fire."

"Where was it?" Daniel asked.

"In the bank—definitely not under my mattress."

Abigail's little boys received puzzles, a new ball, and two used bicycles that had been hidden in the barn when the fire occurred. They were used, but her *dat* had cleaned them up with a coat of paint and new seats.

Abigail and Aaron were given the only thing that actually cost money, and the entire family had pitched in. "A gift card? But..."

"We all contributed, dear." Sarah wrapped an arm around her daughter's shoulder. "It's so you both can pick out what you need for the baby—once you know whether it's another boy or a girl."

"Danki," Aaron said. "We didn't expect that."

There was a surprise for Becca's parents, as well. They all had to troop over to the barn to see it.

"Oh, my." Sarah's fingertips covered her mouth. Sitting in the middle of the room were two rocking chairs.

"For the new front porch, once the house is rebuilt." Abigail put a hand on her stomach.

When it seemed her *mamm* and *dat* still didn't know what to say, Clyde stepped forward. "We didn't waste money on them. Don't worry about that. We found them in town, at a garage sale. The guy had heard about our fire and insisted on giving them to us. We all spent a little time out here the last few days refinishing them."

"Danki," her father said. "This was very thoughtful, and it helps us…"

He swiped at his eyes, then smiled at his family. "It helps us to focus on what's to come rather than what we've lost."

He stared at the ground a moment, then looked up at his family. "I hope you all know that we thank *Gotte* every day for your safety. That house on the hill that's simply a charred ruin now...it doesn't matter. What matters is each person in this room."

Becca felt as if her heart were being wrung like a dish towel. Why was it that her heart felt so tender? Watching her parents, her siblings, even Daniel, reminded her that she'd been focused on the wrong things for too long.

She realized with a start that she didn't feel poor. Their circumstances hadn't changed, not really, but she felt very wealthy.

Her somber thoughts were interrupted by Hannah and Isabelle shouting, "Now for Daniel's present."

"But I didn't get you all anything."

"Because we told you not to, Daniel. Because you're giving us a place to stay." Becca's *mamm* reached over and squeezed his arm. "That gift means more than any other ever could."

Clyde, Hannah and Isabelle had run to one of the back stalls. Now they walked out with a long box holding Daniel's gift.

"I believe I saw that box under my bed."

"*Ya*, it was there, but we had to move it. Didn't want you finding it." Francine ran her fingers up and down her *kapp* strings. "I hope you like it."

"I'm sure I will." Daniel glanced at Becca, his eyes questioning, but she only shrugged. She wasn't going to spoil the surprise now.

He opened the box to reveal a brand-new dark gray horse blanket with the word *Constance* embroidered across the bottom.

"In case we have a cold front, and she needs it."

"Everyone knows how much you care for the horse."

"It was at Lydia Kline's, being embroidered the night of the fire."

Becca heard all the comments from her family, but her attention was on Daniel. Were those tears in his eyes? Over a horse blanket?

But of course, it was more than that. It was that they had, out of their poverty, found a way to give to him. Which was what neighbors and friends were supposed to do. The only question was whether Daniel Glick was merely a friend and neighbor, or did she want him to be more?

Later that evening, when once again she couldn't sleep, Becca made her way to the kitchen. When she saw Daniel sitting there at the table, she almost backed away.

"Please. Don't leave on my account."

"I didn't mean to interrupt you. I didn't think anyone else would be here."

"I was sort of hoping you wouldn't be able to sleep."

"Is that so?"

"Came out wrong." He tapped his journal, then looked up at her and smiled. "What I mean is, I was hoping to have a chance to be alone with you for a few minutes."

"My family is *wunderbaar,* but there are a lot of them."

Daniel was sitting at the end of the table. He nudged the chair closest to him out with his foot, then nodded toward the platter on the table. "There's still a few pieces of chocolate cake left. You know you want one."

"Only if there's cold milk to go with it."

"There is."

"You talked me into it, then."

It felt good to banter back and forth, but Becca knew that she needed to apologize for her earlier behavior. It was too hard living in the same house, dancing around one another, and feeling guilty for her rudeness. Best to clear the air.

She sat across from him and accepted the piece of cake he'd cut for her. Suddenly, she couldn't imagine eating a bite.

Her stomach was doing somersaults. Why did she turn into a silly *youngie* when she was around Daniel? What was it about the way he looked at her that sent her feelings soaring and her pulse thumping?

Was that love?

If it was, how did people live with it over an extended period of time? She felt as if she could run a race, and as if she might be sick, all at the same time.

"Don't you want it?"

"Maybe later." She cleared her throat, stared at the glass of milk, then dared to look up into Daniel's eyes. She'd expected a wide range of responses from him—pity, anger, acceptance, even a brotherly friendship. Yes, he'd said he loved her and wanted to marry her, but after the way she'd acted, she rather suspected that offer had been withdrawn.

Now, as she looked at the man sitting across from her, she saw only love in his eyes, and it humbled her more than anything else that had happened to date.

He set aside his journal. Under it was a plainly wrapped gift with a bright blue ribbon. "This is for you."

"But you weren't supposed to buy us gifts. You're giving enough just letting us live here."

"I bought this before the fire." He pushed it across the table, leaving his fingertips on the edge of the package.

As she reached for it, she was taken aback by the image before her—his hand, her hand, both holding a Christmas gift.

They were so different, and it was evident even in their hands. Daniel's was calloused from hard work, tanned even in the winter, with small scratches here and there.

Hers was smaller, her skin softer and younger.

And the gift? It was probably some simple thing—she hoped it was. Yet she understood that gifts had a way of binding people together.

"Aren't you going to open it?"

"*Ya.* Sure." She'd received a book on raising backyard chickens from her siblings. She hadn't expected anything else. Any other year, she might have felt depressed that their gifts were so few. This year, it hardly mattered.

She untied the ribbon and set it aside. It was long enough to braid in Hannah or Isabelle's hair. She pulled the wrapping paper away and stared at the clothbound book.

"It's a project book."

"Oh."

"For your projects." Daniel scooted closer. "See? Each section is for a different project. There's room for fifty. It includes a place to project costs and materials, then make notations about what works and what doesn't, and finally a cost analysis section."

Becca bit her bottom lip as tears sprang to her eyes. Did he know what this meant to her? He understood her need to help her family. He didn't expect her to wait for a man to swoop in and make everything right. He was no longer suggesting that his money could solve her problems.

"This is very kind. *Danki*, and I'm embarrassed that I don't have a gift for you."

"I didn't expect a gift."

"Daniel, I want to apologize."

"You don't have to do that."

"*Ya.* I do. It was wrong of me to be so angry with you. I was… I guess I was embarrassed. It's been a fear of mine since I was a young child."

"What has been?"

"That people were laughing at me." She shook her head, ran a finger down the binding of the book. "It might have started when I first went to school. Before that, I don't think I realized I was poor. At home, we were all the same. When I went to school, even an Amish school, I realized that my clothes were different— more patched, older, a little too large or a little too small."

"And did they laugh at you, Becca?"

"Maybe. I'm not even sure. I don't remember that part. I only remember how it made me feel, and so I've spent the last few years trying to make sure Hannah and Isabelle don't have to endure the same."

"It's plain how much you and your family care for each other."

"*Mamm* said something to me earlier that caught me by surprise." She thought about admitting that she'd confessed all to her mother, but decided it was best to stay on track. "She told me that she'd never wished for another life. Isn't that amazing?"

"That she has found contentment? It doesn't surprise me. Your *mamm* is a wise woman, Becca. I believe she would be content whether she was rich or poor."

"I thought she was simply putting on a brave front for the rest of us. As for my *dat*, I thought he was simply clueless."

"But he's not."

"*Nein*. It's very clear to me now that he understands what the most important things are—that we have each other, that we're a family, that we put each other and our faith before other things."

Something akin to pain crossed Daniel's features. "If my family understood all of that, I believe they could be happy even with their wealth."

"Which is what I need to apologize for."

"I don't think you do. You were right. I should have been honest with you—maybe not from the first day, but as we became *freinden*."

"Possibly. We can't go back." Becca tugged on her braid, pulled it over her shoulder. "I judged you for being rich, in the same way I was afraid other people had judged me for being poor. I understand now that prejudice goes both ways, and it's wrong. We should see the person, not the bank account behind the person, or what does it mean to be Christian? What does it mean to be Plain? I'm sorry, Daniel. Truly, I am."

"Apology accepted."

Becca worried her bottom lip. She was still nervous but also hungry, so she set the journal aside, loaded a piece of cake on her fork and popped it into her mouth.

Daniel's smile grew, and she knew he was trying to hold back his laughter.

She tried to ask *what?* but it came out as "Wha?" owing to the large piece of cake in her mouth. She managed to swallow, then washed it down with the cold milk. Daniel was still clearly amused.

"Chocolate," he explained, then leaned forward and thumbed the frosting from the corner of her mouth. His hand lingered there, cupping her face.

Becca found herself leaning forward and closing her eyes, and then Daniel's lips were on hers—sweeter than the cake, more tender than a child's fingertips, more precious than any gift she could have received.

Pulling in a deep breath, he rested his forehead against hers.

"I love you. I hope you know that."

"I do."

"Can I ask you again?"

"Yes," she whispered.

"Becca Schwartz, will you marry me?"

"I will."

"You're certain?"

Now she opened her eyes, pulled back and studied him. "I love you, Daniel Glick."

"*Ya?*"

"*Ya.* Don't look so surprised."

"Happy. I'm happy and maybe a little surprised."

"I'm happy, too."

"And you think that you can...accept my life? It's not as easy as you might think, having money."

Her laughter was light and bright and from a place that she'd forgotten existed—a carefree place that trusted things would be okay.

"I know how to be poor."

"You're very good at it."

"I suppose I can learn to be wealthy."

He stood and pulled her into his arms. "We'll love each other all of our days."

"For better or worse."

"For richer or poorer."

Which really was all they needed to say. The details could be worked out another time. They stood in the middle of the kitchen, their arms wrapped around one another, and enjoyed the last few minutes of a very special Christmas, one Becca knew she'd never forget.

Epilogue

Seven months later

Becca stood on the front porch of her house—her and Daniel's house—and shaded her eyes to better see across the yard.

"Looking for Carl-the-bad-tempered-rooster?" Daniel walked up behind her and slipped his arms around her waist.

"How did you know?"

"Because you're frowning."

"That rooster is going to take five years off my life."

"He's out by the road."

"The road?"

"Chasing the mailman."

"He chased the mailman?"

"Don't worry. The mailman was in an *Englisch* car. He made a clean getaway."

She wrapped her arms around his. In the distance, she could make out her *bruder* working in the field alongside her *dat*. By the street was a simple sign that read G&S Organic Farm—Produce and Eggs. The two properties had become one, as had the two families.

From the corner of their porch, she could just see her parents' new home that had been built in the spring—plain, sturdy and paid for by the *freinden* in their community. Daniel had made a large, anonymous donation to the benevolence fund—more than enough to cover the cost of materials. As for the labor, there was no way to repay that except by being willing to help when someone else needed assistance.

Before they were married, she and Daniel had met with the bishop and discussed how to handle their finances. His advice had been remarkably clear and wise.

Live simply.

Help others when you can.

Be grateful.

Becca was surprised that very little in their lives had actually changed. She no longer felt the desperate need to help her parents financially. In fact, her parents were doing quite well. Turned out that her *dat* was a natural at organic farming.

"I passed your *schweschder* on my way down the lane."

"Abigail?"

"*Ya.*"

"Did she bring Baby Tabitha?"

"She did."

Becca spun in Daniel's arms, reached up and touched his face. "Now would be a *gut* time to tell them that we're expecting."

"I was thinking the same thing."

He slipped his hand into hers, and they walked across the property that was bathed in the afternoon's summer sunshine. Becca couldn't help feeling that they were walking into their future.

Together.

* * * * *

Dear Reader,

Have you ever wished you could live a different life? Sometimes we wish we had more money, or lived in a different place, or had made different choices in our past. It's easy to find ourselves living in "what might have been."

Becca Schwartz has very good reasons for wanting to help her family raise their standard of living. She cares about her sisters and brothers. She loves her parents but doesn't understand their lack of concern over their financial situation. Becca believes that having more money will solve every problem that they face.

Daniel Glick understands that money can sometimes cause more problems than it solves. He has watched as what should have been a blessing actually tore his family apart. Instead of realizing that there were problems before the inheritance, he takes a vow of poverty, moves to a different state and tries to live a different life.

Becca and Daniel are more than opposites. They both are trying to overcome something in their life, and neither is ready to accept that God didn't make a mistake giving them the life they have. Neither is able to look past their own fears and hurts to consider what God would have them learn—what God would have them do. It's not an easy thing to trust. It isn't easy for my characters, and sometimes it isn't easy for myself, either.

I hope you enjoyed reading *The Amish Christmas Secret*. I welcome comments and letters at vannettachapman@gmail.com.

May we continue to "always give thanks to God the Father for everything, in the name of our Lord Jesus Christ" (Ephesians 5:20).

Blessings,
Vannetta